A Thorn Among Roses

Hayley Anderton

This book is dedicated to all the people who have never felt truly comfortable in their skin. You are so beautiful. You are so loved.

Playlist

My Mistake - Gabrielle Aplin

The Archer - Taylor Swift

This is Me - Keala Settle

you'd never know - BLU EYES

this is me trying - Taylor Swift

Young and Beautiful - Lana Del Rey

Salvation - Gabrielle Aplin

Anti-Hero - Taylor Swift

The Only Exception - Paramore

Somewhere Along The Road - Emily Smith

Trigger Warnings

Poor self body image and mental health issues, violence, burns and cuts, arachnid creatures, bugs and snakes, physical and verbal cruelty, offensive language regarding appearances, general prejudice, death, death of close family members, trauma, scars, misogyny.

Prologue

Death is waiting at the borders.

I see it with my own eyes as I flee to the woods with my white wolf, Bolt, running close at my heels. My people fighting - and losing - to the creatures swarming the kingdom. Obsidian spider-like creatures thrice my height with pincers sharper than swords, their bodies protected by thick muscular armor. My parents ride into the fray atop their wolves, right into the thick of the hopeless battle. The last thing I see before I turn to run into the woods is a terrible black pincer slicing through my father's body.

Shock makes it almost impossible to breathe. My heavy armor weighs me down even more, so much that I feel as though I am running in place. But I have to get out of here, and fast. I want to stand and fight with my people, but I know that it will only get me killed too. I have to do something to save them. There is no time to think of what I have lost, what I could still lose.

I know what I have to do if I want to save the kingdom. Something my parents were never willing to entertain. I run as hard as I can, my feet avoiding tripping over the thick tree roots that snake across the forest. If I do nothing, the kingdom will be lost. Hundreds will die. And if my mother is lost to the battle too, then I am now the remainder of the monarchy. It falls to me to do what is best for us all.

Even if I will be shunned for it.

There is a witch who lives deep in these trees. She lives so deep in the woods that legend has it her home has been swallowed up by the trees and vines. They say she is a thousand years old, that she remembers a time when magic ruled and wasn't exiled into the trees. They say that the trees remember too and keep her safe, even now. My mother and father allowed her to keep living in the depths of our lands so long as she did no harm. And now, she may be the only one who can save us.

I only hope I can find her.

Bolt howls as thorns snag at her fur, but continues to run beside me. She's only a pup, still unfamiliar with the lay of our land. But I've grown up here in the embrace of nature. I know it well, even in the woods left largely unexplored, allowed to grow wild untouched. Outsiders find these dark woods scary, but I am well aware that much more terrifying things lie beyond our borders. Now they have come calling, and only I can stop it.

Breathless, I spy the place I've been seeking. The stone cottage has truly accepted the embrace of the woods, thick moss growing on the roof and heavy branches of oak trees bowing over it. The land is untamed here, as though no one has walked through it in many years.

And yet somebody remains here. Through a dusty window, I see a figure hunched over a table by candlelight. It has to be the witch I'm looking for. The witch known to townsfolk as Laurel, as a whisper of trouble, a bad omen. I can only pray to the goddess Selene that this is the right choice.

"Wait here," I whisper to Bolt as I approach the cabin without hesitation. I cannot afford to wait around and find my courage. I must simply have it. Bolt whines behind me, but I ignore her and knock on the cabin door.

"Enter, child," a gravelly voice instructs me. I refuse to pay any mind to the shaking of my hands as I push open the door.

The cabin is strange. It's musty and cold, but I can also smell sweet flowers underneath the bad smells. Mushrooms are growing almost everywhere I look, on the walls and the ground. There are skeletons of dead flowers in a vase at the table the witch sits at. She smiles at me and for whatever reason, it makes my blood run cold.

The witch may be thousands of years old, but she doesn't look like it. Then again it's hard to tell because she's so unusual. Green eyed and pale skinned with long brown hair…nothing too unusual about that. But it's the small details that make me uneasy. There are twigs tangled in her hair and a snake has settled around her neck like a scarf. She has allowed the woods to dress her, covering her body in mud and moss. My breath hitches when I see bugs skittering across her skin, but she doesn't blink an eye. It seems this is the witch's norm. Beneath the muck, golden tattoos swirl over her skin. The marks of the goddess, Cressida, the mother of every witch ever to live. The witch is both beautiful and terrifying all at once.

"Queen Alana of Thornwood. I have been waiting for you," Laurel says to me. I swallow back nerves.

"I am no queen."

"You are now," the witch says, her mouth twisting. My heart squeezes hard. I have had no time to process that my father has been struck down…and now my mother too? The thought brings me to my knees, my hand pressing to my breastplate.

"Don't fret, child. The creatures will soon cleanse the land of humanity. Your people will not feel pain for much longer."

"No," I choke. "You have to help. That is why I came to you."

Laurel chuckles quietly. "It does tend to be the way, does it not? The kingdom seeks the shunned witch every time they need saving from something they are too weak to face themselves. I have met many of your ancestors, Alana. They all promised me a better world if I helped them. And yet I have remained in these woods for longer than you can even begin to fathom."

I swallow. "I am not like them."

"Until you are."

"No," I say firmly. "I do not believe there is any benefit in hiding magic away. The goddesses would never approve. Not after they blessed so few with their powers. I would see the return of magic to our lands…if it were up to me."

Laurel's eyebrow quirks just a little. Perhaps I have surprised her. She leans forward at her table, looking down at my kneeling place.

"Perhaps I have misjudged you. Perhaps not. What is it that you want?"

"Only to save my people. I will do anything," I plead. "I just want to keep my kingdom safe. That is my job now. That is all that is left for me. I am the end of the line. Without a queen to protect the kingdom, everyone will die."

"You poor thing. Bound by duty," Laurel says, but there is no trace of sympathy in her voice. There is a subtle cruelty to her, like her heart has become as twisted as the tree roots engulfing her home. "You will do anything?"

I raise my eyes to meet her gaze. Outside, I can hear Bolt howling, as though she's telling me no. But I don't have time to consider if this is a bad idea. Every second I wait, my people are being slaughtered. We have already lost too much.

"I can give you power...I can give you invincibility," Laurel murmurs. "You will single-handedly be able to defeat every single creature at the borders without bearing a scratch. But it will come at a price."

"I will bear it," I say firmly. Laurel smiles.

"You do not know what it is."

"I said I will bear it."

Laurel rises from her seat, standing taller than I thought possible for a person. But she is no ordinary woman. She looks down on me as though I am a field mouse and she is a hawk about to swallow me whole.

"So be it, Alana. I shall bestow the curse upon you now. You will be granted twenty-four hours to end this battle once and for all before your skin once again becomes penetrable. But be warned, child. Only the most powerful magic in this world will break the curse that will remain with you afterward. Only a kiss from your true love will free you."

"Please. Just do it," I say, barely registering what she is telling me. Nothing matters but saving all those people dying at my borders. My sacrifice, whatever it is, will be worth it. It has to be. She steps toward me once again and places a long dirty nail under my chin.

"Brave child," she murmurs. Then she clutches my head hard, making me cry out in surprise. There is heat in her palms like I've never felt in skin to skin contact. It burns to the point where it feels as though my skin should be melting away, but still she holds me in place, her grip as strong as iron.

She begins to murmur under her breath, her words too rapid for me to understand. Some enchantment, I presume. I find that I am shaking, as much as I do not want to. I want to seem brave, though I am far from it. I still feel like a child. I am not ready for this.

But if I am the final hope, then I refuse to back down. I cannot stand to see any more death. I grit my teeth as the pain intensifies to the point where I am blinded by it. And when it finally stops, I blink several times, my legs shaking. I try to stand and almost fall down. Laurel chuckles to herself, turning her back on me dismissively.

"Go, child. Your kingdom awaits. But do not forget about me. I will remember your promises to me. Magic shall return to our lands…or on your head be it."

I stumble from the cabin, barely listening to her words. I have to end this now. Bolt howls at me as I trip forward and break into a run. At first, I am unsteady on my feet like a newborn deer, but as I continue to run, I feel energy coursing through my veins, bringing me to life like never before. I feel weightless, my heavy armor no longer slowing me down. This has to be a part of the gift Laurel has bestowed upon me. I run harder and faster than I thought possible. I have already been gone for far too long. My people need me.

As I reach the borders of the vine wall that encases Thornwood, I see the carnage that has unfolded. People lie dead all around me. People that I have known since I was a child, people loyal to the crown, people who were unprepared for this. My throat is tight, but I know I cannot bring them back. I can only save the living now.

Terror twists my stomach as I see the obsidian spiders still terrorizing the fighting townsfolk. The people of Thornwood are no match for these monsters, and they are starting to realize it. Some are retreating back to the town, where the spiders have yet to reach. The borders are strong, made of thick, tall vines and roots. They have kept Thornwood from harm so far. But if I want to stop these creatures from getting inside the kingdom, then I must be the one to go forward and end this.

I have to trust that Laurel has truly given me the power of invincibility, or this battle will soon end for me. I draw my sword and Bolt howls once again, knowing what this means.

"Bolt, go home!" I cry out as I run. She whines for a moment, but when I bark the order a second time, she runs off. I have already lost my parents. I cannot love my beloved pup too.

And now that all distractions are gone, I throw myself into the battle.

I am soon surrounded by the tall spindled legs of the monsters. I quickly assess what I am dealing with. The weak points appear to be the legs and the underbelly of the creatures. No wonder so many are dying trying to kill them - it's near impossible to reach these points without sustaining an injury. But I put faith in

Laurel's magic, and it cannot fail me here. I let out a battle cry as I make my first slice, my sword cutting deep into the leg of one of the creatures. It lets out a terrifying hissing noise, turning its attention to me. It swipes at me with one of its pincers, grabbing my body and lifting me up. It squeezes the pincer tighter and tighter, making panic rise inside me. It should be crushing me right now, should be stealing the air from my lungs. But the pincer doesn't even dent my armor. The witch has made good on her word.

And now I am face to face with this thing, I know what to do. I manage to get my sword out on the grip of the pincer and plunge it into the eye of the monster. It lets out a scream and its grip on me loosens, dropping me to the ground. I land with a thud, but I am unharmed. I do not feel a thing. I rise to my feet once again, gritting my teeth. The battle will be long and arduous, but I can do this. I can end this.

With a cry of rage, I continue to fight.

Many hours have passed me by. The sky turns dark and I continue my onslaught, alone on the battlefield with a hundred creatures trying to kill me. The townsfolk have disappeared to their homes, allowing me to continue my deadly dance without their help. But my body does not tire. I am drowning in the thick black blood of my enemies, but nothing will stop me. By the light of the moon, I chip away at the monsters, telling myself that this will all be worth it. What is twenty-four hours of my life versus saving a thousand lives?

The ground beneath my feet is wet with blood and rainwater, keeping the mud around me slippery, but it is more of a disadvantage to the creatures than it is to me. They claw at me, knock me aside, try to crush me with their pincers, but none of their tricks are working for them. I bat their advances away with my impenetrable armor and then sweep beneath their bellies to secure each kill. I am unstoppable. They surround me in one black mass, but I fight tooth and nail, doing what I must to put an end to this. I feel almost drunk on my heightened emotions - the rage, the fear, the agony of knowing how many lives were lost before I got here. I want to stop and weep. I want to bury myself in Bolt's fur and let exhaustion consume me. But I will not falter. This is all or nothing.

And I cannot allow this to be for nothing.

The numbers of the creatures dwindle slowly as the sun rises. My progress is slow, but constant. These mindless beasts seem intent on taking me down, and they have lost their focus on the town that lies just beyond the borders. But nothing they do can touch me for now. Time is trickling away from me, but so long as the magic remains, I can keep fighting.

Few of the creatures remain. I lash out with might I have never possessed before and will never possess again. There can be no giving up now when I am so close to victory. I slide a little on the murky ground, delving my sword once again into the underbelly of a horrifying creature. My sword comes back out black as it dies, its corpse still towering over me as I back up to take on the final few.

I know that my time is close to ending. If I do not finish them soon, it will all be for nothing. I will die and the monsters will tear up the kingdom. I raise my sword once again, breathing hard, preparing myself for the final onslaught.

"I will not surrender!" I cry out as the creatures advance upon me. They have been coming from miles around and they are the final frontier. Let them come. Let them try to smite me after what they have taken from me.

They will not succeed.

I cry out as I run forth and mount the spindly leg of one of the creatures. I slice the tip of its leg, watching it topple sideways as I leap from my perch upon it. I finish it off with a stab in its underside and move on before another can attack me. One slides its pincer toward me, trying to snap me up, but I swipe up a fallen sword and wedge it between the pincers, confusing the creature for long enough that I can run beneath its body and attack the weak spot. I am pure adrenaline and nothing more.

Until I feel the feeling begin to slip away from me. I look to the sky and know that my time is up. I turn just in time to see one final creature scuttling my way.

It is too late for me to stop the attack. I cry out as the pincer slices through my face. Warm blood begins to run down my face like deadly tears. My body is beginning to shake. The magic is gone. If the creature hits me again now, I will surely die.

Exhaustion is consuming me too fast, but I have to end this. I slice desperately at the legs of the monster, all too aware that magic is no longer my shield and savior. I have to rely on the skills I grew up with, the training that prepared me for battle. Sword at the ready, I make my move.

I shoulder forward, blocking the enemy's pincer with my padded shoulder. The pincer is strong and crumples my armor. Pain jolts through my arm socket, but I allow my cry of pain to fuel me forward. Like I have done a thousand times tonight, I need to get beneath the creature and skewer the underbelly.

The shadow of its huge body engulfs me into near darkness, but I am at the finish line. With one final cry, I plunge my sword up into the underbelly of the creature. It squeals, its cry long and thin. The final call of battle. I pull back my sword, leaping aside as the creature falls down. I hit the ground, closing my eyes. I'm panting for breath, my bleeding face pressed into the dirt. The silence that ensues, quiet after so many hours, shakes me to my core.

It is over. It is finally over.

I do not know how long I lie in the blood and the mud, catching my breath, feeling exhaustion setting into my bones. But it is over. I did it.

It takes me a long time to regain the energy to prop myself up by my sword and stagger back into the kingdom's borders, leaving behind the graveyard of monsters and humans alike. Among the masses, I cannot even see my parents or their wolves. Tears fall now, settling into the deep wound on my face. But I am alive. Others must be too. All is not lost, even if it feels as though it is.

I walk the streets where the townsfolk are hiding. Slowly, they begin to come out of their houses, fear laced in their expressions. I fall to my knees, too exhausted to continue, but I know I must address these people. I am their queen now, whether I like it or not. My body trembles as the crowds gather to see me crumpled before them, completely spent. I look around at them, the wound on my face throbbing.

"The battle is won…but the king and queen fell," I tell them all, tears falling from my face. "But you are safe again. I vow that I will continue to keep you all safe…as I take on my reign."

There is silence in the crowd. I wonder if it is shock that keeps them quiet. But then an older man shuffles forward, staring at me in contempt.

"How did you defeat them all alone?" he asks. "And barely a scratch on you…"

"It is the work of magic," a bitter faced woman declares, glaring at me. "She is cursed."

My shoulders sag. "It was the only way. The battle was lost….I had to do what was best for my people."

"Your parents never would have given in to magic. Not after it destroyed our ancestors' lives. How magic pummeled them all into the ground," the woman sneers.

"That is our history, not our future. We would not be alive now if not for the witch who aided me…"

"You dared to deal with Laurel? She refused to stop practicing magic. That is why she was exiled. How could you turn to her in our hour of need?" the woman snaps. I stare at her in disbelief.

"What would you have had me do? Leave you all to die? You all ran and hid within your homes. Did you believe that would keep you safe?" I say, desperation in my voice. No one dares reply at first. They know there is sense in what I am saying. But the more I look around, the more I see how much these people hate what I did. I see the disgust in their eyes. I see that they are happy to be unreasonable to fit the purpose of their argument.

"You should never have allowed this to happen! It is unnatural! Magic has no place here!" another voice cries. My forehead creases.

"The goddesses themselves bestowed magic on the witch who helped me! Do we not trust in their power? We should be grateful!"

"We shall never be grateful! Those creatures were born of magic too. Did you ever stop to think about that?" the old man snaps at me. He steps closer to where I kneel hopelessly on the ground, poking at me with his walking stick. "And now you are tainted by magic too. I watched what you did. How you took hit after hit without any harm befalling you. It is horrifying. You are barely human…you are a beast!"

Cries of agreement surge from the crowd. The man grins down at me with crooked teeth and bats me down once again with his stick. I scramble away, trying to get to my feet. I am weak with exhaustion and dizzied by the sudden turning of the tides, but I know I must leave. I begin to run for the castle, my heart pounding hard in my chest.

"That's right! Run away, Cursed Queen!" the bitter woman cries out. "You may rule these lands, but you will never rule us!"

I run until I think I might collapse. I run up and up the hill back toward the castle where I have always resided. A castle fit for a queen, but not one such as me.

I do not make it home before I tumble to the ground in exhaustion once again, feeling rain beginning to fall on my face. I cannot move. I feel the dirt around me turn to mud, but still I stay. After some time I hear a gentle whine and something nudging my face. Bolt has come to find me. The only one left who does not see me as a monster.

And as I lie here, I feel the curse taking hold. I feel the moment when my skin melds with my breastplate, locking it to my chest. I watch as my armor transforms and metal spikes begin to protrude from it like thorns on a rose stem. A warning to all to stay away from me. And now I understand that this curse is designed to stop the only thing that can break it - to stop someone from getting close, to stop them falling in love.

Only now do I see how cruel Laurel truly is.

It feels like days until I have the strength to make it back to the castle, dripping wet, but I no longer feel the rain on my skin, the cold seeping into my bones. In fact, I feel very little at all. The curse is taking what is left of my humanity, devoting me of all feeling. Another step to making me unlovable.

In the castle, there is not a soul around. I stumble to my bedroom to examine myself in the mirror.

And staring back at me is someone I do not recognize. I may still have the same broad shoulders, tall stature, russet red hair, but the rest of me has changed. Blood has crusted on my face around the deep gash. My armor has embedded into my body, seamlessly becoming one with my skin. I reach up to touch my face and the scar that runs from between my brows to my cheek and onto my neck. My only reminder of everything I fought so hard for, for what I sacrificed.

Only for me to be shunned by my people.

One thing slowly becomes clear to me. I may be the queen of these lands, but I will never be accepted or loved by these people. I will never earn their trust after what I did, and I will never be forgiven. I have made my bed so now I must lie in it.

And above all, I will never escape my curse.

For no one will ever fall in love with a beast like me.

Chapter One

When you have worn a curse for long enough, you become a curse yourself.

It has been three years since I saved Thornwood from the darkest creatures ever to come to our borders. It has been three years since I lost both of my parents and was forced to step up as the queen. And it has been three years of loneliness, three years of learning that no matter my sacrifices, my people now only see me as a monster.

I am a restless creature these days. I walk the halls of my dark and dusty castle with Bolt at my feet, wondering how this place fell so far from grace. The day I returned from battle covered in blood, but none of it my own, the servants fled from me, leaving me alone in this place. I did not try to find others to replace them. I figured it would be best to stick this out alone.

But how do you stick something out when

there is no end to it? I have nobody to speak to. I talk to Bolt just to make sure I do not lose my voice forever. I never receive visitors, though my only purpose is to serve the people of my kingdom. No one came on my crowning day. My subjects cowered in the town away from me, and I began to understand the sacrifice I made. I did everything I could to save them from the beasts, and now I am the beast that has taken their place.

I do not eat. I do not sleep. The curse keeps me alive no matter how much I neglect my body. I am trapped within this metal shell with no end in sight. I try to keep myself busy. I spend long nights reading by candlelight in the library, escaping to realities better than my own. In the day, I walk through my gardens with Bolt at my side, or chop wood to send down to the villagers, or pray to the goddess for reprieve at the edge of the woods. But lately, the goddess has not been answering my prayers. Perhaps she too has given up on me.

I only have myself to blame, and yet I am willing to place the blame wherever I feel like it on any given day. I blame the villagers and their cowardice. I blame the witch for luring me in with such a cruel promise. I blame my parents for not being stronger, for forcing my hand when they died on the battlefield. Sometimes I have to blame them just to push down my bitter thoughts. If I do not blame myself, then I can pretend that none of this is my fault.

Perhaps I am a beast after all.

This morning is cool and misty. Bolt loves this weather, and I cannot deny her small pleasures, so I pull on my old leather boots and head out into the gardens with her. My boots have holes in them and the leather is worn, but my request for new ones from the shoemaker in the village was refused. Though I have plenty of gold, the townsfolk refuse to take it or help me in any way. It is fortunate that I do not need anything from them to keep myself alive, or I would have been in trouble long ago.

As much as the state of my boots bothers me, as water squelches through to my feet I barely feel it. Ever since the curse was bestowed upon me, everything I feel has been muted. Even the pain of loneliness feels like a dull ache, almost unreachable to me some days. There is a disconnect within me that I have been unable to fix. I have given up trying.

Bolt splashes her way through the muddied grounds, howling to the sky as thunder crackles overhead. I watch her play in the overgrown, boggy stretch of land and envy her. She plays like a child and I see the joy it brings her. I wish that life could be so simple for me again. I wish

I could live that way. If I truly were a beast, I could run alongside Bolt, and she would not fear me as the townsfolk do. We could disappear into the woods forever and never look back.

Still, I endure this lonely existence in this castle. The curse rests bitter in my heart, somewhere beneath my thorned breastplate. And until I receive a kiss from my true love, I cannot escape this fate.

Now I understand why the witch told me it would be near impossible to break. How could anyone ever fall in love with me now? A woman with armor melded to her skin, thorns keeping anyone at bay who tries to get too close. A woman who can barely feel, who is left with only the memories of everything she gave up for people who turned their back on her. I am jaded, I am cold and I am impossible to love. These three years alone have taught me that.

I slosh through the mud, rain bouncing off my armor and soaking my hair. I should make myself useful. Most days, I head out into the woods with an axe to make the most of my time, chopping wood to fuel the fires in the homes of the townspeople. But on days like today, I do not feel much like helping anyone. Not when the merchant who collects the wood from me refuses to meet my eyes and neglects to pay me for my labor. Not when the people I provide for have so much unnecessary hate in their hearts for me. So today, I will walk across my land and try to count my blessings. There are worse places to live out my exile than in a castle.

Bolt rounds the side of the stone building that I have always called home. It is starting to fall to ruin these days, and ivy threads itself into every nook between the bricks. Thunder claps once more overhead, lighting the sky and my home. I can see from this angle that it looks like the perfect place for someone like me to reside. A derelict building is the perfect host for such a monster.

I follow Bolt's paw prints. The rain shows no signs of letting up - the goddess seems keen to keep my rose garden watered. Roses have long grown in Thornwood castle. They are the sigil of our kingdom, the flower that reminds us to be gentle people to please the goddess. But the thorns have meaning too - they remind outsiders that we protect our own, supposedly. Though I am not sure that applies to me any longer. I protect myself, I protect my people, but they do not do the same in return.

I walk over to the bushes and place one of my fingers on the bud of a deep red rose. It is almost the same color as my hair. I can remember my mother making the comparison when I was a child. I swallow, not wanting to think of her. I pluck a flower to take with me back to the castle. Something beautiful to take my focus away from how I have allowed my home to go to ruin. My finger brushes along one of the thorns, but I do not wince, not even when a bead of blood appears on my fingertip. I close my fist around the stems and the thorns dig into my hand, but I feel nothing. The curse has gone deeper than any flower could ever root. I sometimes wonder if I will ever feel fully again. It scares me to imagine that I may not.

I abandon the flower on the grass and continue my walk. The day is young, and yet I am already craving the moment where night comes and I can declare it over.

The storm ends as the night draws in. Bolt and I head back inside the castle, the cold barely touching either of us. Bolt shakes her fur and pants, looking pleased with herself as mud speckles the stone floors. I bend down beside her to scruff her fur.

"It is a good job we are not expecting guests, is it not?" I murmur to her. She lets out a short whine and rubs her face against mine. I close my eyes, my throat suddenly tight. I may be mostly alone, but I feel lucky that I still have her. Bolt has always been able to read my emotions. She may not be able to speak, but I know she understands me as well as I understand her. Her rough tongue slurps up my neck to make me laugh, and it works. I wrestle with her and she lets out a deep bark, a sparkle in her eyes. Even with the thorns protruding from my armor, she never shies away from me. This is the closest I get to feeling anything, with my loyal pup at my side.

But at night, that is when the world gets too quiet. Bolt sleeps at the front of the castle, keeping guard and leaving me to my own devices. Tonight, I light a candle and climb the stone staircase, my lonely footsteps echoing through the halls. There is only one place for a night like this, with rain dripping down the window panes and sadness resting in my heart.

The library opens itself up to me. It is the place that gives me some reprieve from the world. My father in particular loved to read, and he had books imported from lands far and wide - epic adventure volumes from Riverhold, historic texts from the world's largest library in Highcourt, scorched parchments with strange mythology from Emberstone. He once told me that if duty did not call to him, he would spend all of his time reading. Now I have nothing but time, and I feel that I must make time for the books he never got to finish.

Reading is a small pleasure in a miserable existence here. I plan to read every book in this room someday, but for now, I am reading about love. It makes me quietly hopeful. Love was something I always thought would stumble upon me some day, sweeping me away to experience life beyond my expectations as a princess. But since I have become the queen I have learned that love will not come easily to me, no matter how much I wish it. So I read about it instead. I am halfway through a fat volume about two women falling in love in a coastal town a thousand miles from here. It is more than enough to sweep me away.

I lose myself in the pages for a while. This is the time when my heart steadies and I forget what I have become. It doesn't feel as though my eyes are scanning a page. I am absorbed, hours passing me by before I even know that time is slipping away from me. I turn the page, realizing I am only a few chapters from the end…

And that is when I'm snapped back to reality.

Bolt's howl echoes through the night. I stand immediately, rushing to her. She never has cause to howl in the night unless she senses trouble. Nothing much bothers us up here, so the sound of her voice sends me spiraling into terror.

I hurtle down the stairs and see over the bannister that Bolt is unharmed, but something has caught her eye out of the window.

"What is it, girl?" I urge as I rush to her side. Out of the window, in the misty night, I see something that makes my breath hitch.

A fire. I squint my eyes. Somebody has pitched a tent on my grounds and made a campfire. Who would dare get this close to the castle?

Only someone who does not come from here. An outsider.

I know I have to go out there and face whoever it is. I grab my heavy battle axe from my weapons rack in the hallway. I haven't had much cause to use it in recent years, but I have only grown stronger in my solitude, training just to pass the time, swinging an axe almost every day. Whoever is trespassing will soon regret that decision.

"Let us go and greet our guests," I murmur.

Chapter Two

I trudge out into the night. I can hear laughter and talking at the campsite. Perhaps they don't even know I am here, but they soon will. All these years alone have made me especially wary of company, especially when I did not invite them here. Do they not know that they are trespassing on royal land?

I can make out three figures in the dark, sitting around the campfire with a tent behind them. There are two women and a man, the three of them laughing loudly at something. Four horses wander aimlessly, grazing on the muddy grass.

The people do not notice my arrival. They hold flagons of ale in their hands. Perhaps that is the source of their ignorance, drunk beyond reason.

"You should not be here," I growl as I approach. The three of them leap to their feet in surprise, the man spilling from his flagon as he stumbles. But still, he grins at me as though we are old friends.

"Greetings, stranger! We mean you no harm. We were told this was a good place to set up camp. Did we steal your camping spot?"

"You are trespassing on my land. Do you not know what that is behind me?" I hiss, pointing at the castle. "You are speaking with Queen Alana of Thornwood."

The man's face quickly fades to horror and he drops to one knee, bowing his head. "I…I do apologize, your majesty. I swear, we meant no harm. The villagers told us we could set up our camp here for a few days…they claimed no one lives in the castle. We are travelers…we have no idea that Thornwood was still ruled by a queen."

I ball my hands into fists. If I wasn't so despised by my own people, I might have chosen not to believe his story. Unfortunately for me, it is easily believable. But what is left of my pride puts me on the defensive. I make a show of swinging my axe to rest on my shoulder, making the man's eyes bulge in terror.

"Your little story seems very convenient. You expect me to believe that you thought you could simply *camp* on royal land?"

The man blinks several times, trying to think of something to say. But that is when I see the tent flap move and another woman comes out to greet me.

"There is no need for violence here," she says, her voice quiet as a whisper, but utterly enthralling. I forget that I am supposed to be angry for a moment as the stranger comes into view.

The beauty of the woman takes me by surprise. I know immediately that she is from a place far, far from here, from a place where magic is said to have been born. I have heard of the witches of Celestia from books that I have read, but the only one I have ever met is Laurel, and she does not compare to the sight of this young woman.

The bodies of witches are blessed by the goddess of the sky, Cressida, leaving them with swirling golden tattoos on their skin. Their goddess is said to have once been a star, and when she burned out, she fell to this world as stardust, transforming the women of Celestia into the witches they are known as today. Thousands of years ago, they began to venture out to the rest of the world, taking magic with them. Now, witches live all over the world, and some worship other goddesses, but if you ask anyone the origin of magic, they will tell you about Celestia.

I have no doubt that this woman came from

there. This woman's skin is darker than the golden markings on her arms, her neck, her legs, but her flesh is still tinged with gold. Her eyes are so dark they're almost black, but it is impossible to miss the flecks of gold in her irises. Her hair is trimmed close to her head, but this too is golden, flat and silky against her skull. I can only imagine how she would look in the sunlight, her tattoos shimmering on her skin, her eyes lighting up in the sun.

I blink away my thoughts. What is wrong with me? She is a witch. I should kill her where she stands. The last witch I came in contact with cursed me. Granted, I allowed her to, but she had no interest in helping me. She just wanted to inflict misery on the remainder of the family who exiled her. It is the very reason I went back on my promises to help her. She can stay in exile as far as I am concerned.

"Please do not jump to any conclusions about how to deal with this situation," the witch says, bringing me back to the present.. "Allow me to introduce myself and my friends. My name is Fiora. This here is Neville," she says pointing to the man who still looks scared out of his wits. "He is our cook. And this," she says nodding to the shorter woman with a freckled face. "Is Sigrid. She keeps us entertained on the road with her lute."

Sigrid shrugs. Her hair is half shorn at the side and she has piercings that shoot through her ears, her nose, her lips. "I try."

"And this is her wife, Calla. She makes us laugh."

Calla chuckles a little nervously. She bears a dark birthmark that dips between her eyebrows and beneath her right eye. She has blue eyes so bright that I can see them in the dark.

The three of them are eyeing me up anxiously. Only Fiora seems unafraid of me. I guess she doesn't need to be, considering that she is a witch. She is more powerful than me and she knows it.

"And you practice magic," I say, glaring at her. She may not be from around here, but she should know that magic is outlawed almost everywhere, especially in the east. It has been for many years. She may be powerful, but she is limited by it. She may be capable of doing amazing things, but she would be prosecuted for them if the wrong people caught her.

"I am capable of magic…but I only use it when necessary, or when asked to," Fiora says calmly. "And I sense you are no stranger to magic, your majesty. In fact, I think you know magic beyond anything I have ever seen. A witch with powers beyond anything I have ever known cursed you, did she not?"

I take a step back, on the defensive. "How could you possibly know that?"

"Magic knows magic," she replies. She does not shy away from my gaze, locking me in place with her. "Perhaps I could help you. If you can help us. We came to camp here because there are few places for us to go right now. Calla twisted her ankle on the road, and we sorely need to stop and recoup. If you are willing, perhaps you could open your doors to us. In return, I will do what I can to help rid you of your curse. Does that sound fair to you?"

I stare at her in shock. It has been a long while since I received an offer of help. In fact, the very last time I received help, it ended up in the curse I bear. I feel wary of this woman and her intentions. What can she possibly stand to gain if she aids me?

"I assure you, I do not have ulterior motives," Fiora says, her voice always level no matter how the conversation seems to flow. "It seems that we can both benefit from one another if you are willing to accept the offer."

"You are trespassers. You broke the law."

"I understand. But if you accept this bargain, I will have to break it again. It will take strong magic to free you of the curse you bear, I feel. But I am willing to try if you can shelter us until it is done. Do we have a deal?"

I narrow my eyes at the beautiful witch. I do not like the idea of trusting her. Magic has only ever brought sorrow to my life. But at this point, do I have anything else to lose? I am already a recluse, cursed to live my days alone. Perhaps if nothing else, these people can provide some company for a short while.

My loneliness gets the better of me. I take a deep breath and reach out my hand for the witch to shake. She forces a pleasant smile upon her face and takes my hand. I almost gasp as our skin touches for the first time. I can *feel* it. My fingertips buzz with sensation. How can this be? The curse took feeling from me, rendering me numb all over. And yet suddenly, this witch has brought it all rushing back. I try to control my breathing. This should not be possible.

And yet it seems it is.

"It is settled," Fiora says with a nod. "May we come inside?"

I shoot a glance at Neville, who still looks horrified by me. I almost sigh. At this point, I am used to being looked at as though I am a monster. He is no exception to the rule. I simply turn my back on them all and begin to walk back up to the castle.

"You may sleep wherever you please. Just do not disturb me," I say. Bolt runs along beside me, her face inquisitive as we head back inside, but I have no answers to her silent questions. Why would I allow these people to stay? It has to go beyond the bargain we struck, that much I can admit to myself. Would I have felt differently if Fiora was not a part of the deal? I think I would.

One thing I am certain about is that I am curious about her. Something about her pulls me in. And if she can bring sensations back to my body that I thought had abandoned me forever, then I cannot let her leave so quickly.

Perhaps she is the answer to all of my prayers.

Chapter Three

I have grown too used to being alone, and now the castle seems far too loud. As my strange new guests make themselves at home in the empty rooms, their voices echo through the night, making me flinch each time I hear them. It has been so long since I heard a voice other than my own that it feels like an invasion. I have spent so many years wishing for company, but now that it is here, I guess I have changed my mind.

Fiora is the last to enter the castle, her clothing damp and tight on her slim frame. I blush, looking away. The last thing I need is for this witch to see me looking at her. She must get that wherever she goes. She stands out from the crowd.

I guess we both have that in common.

"Is there somewhere we can go? Somewhere I can take a look at what I am dealing with?" she asks. Her voice is sweet like honey, silky as it leaves her mouth. I swallow. Does she have this effect on everyone she meets, or is it just me?

"I will show you to your bedroom. You can take a look there," I say bluntly, already turning my back on her and heading for the stairs. I hear her following me so I don't bother to turn until I hear her giggling. I whip my head around and see that Bolt is bounding along beside her, her tongue lapping at Fiora's gold dusted hands. I narrow my eyes. *Some guard dog you are,* I think to myself. It only makes me more certain that the witch has some kind of magic to draw others in, to make them feel comfortable and safe around her. That has to be the explanation for how she has made me feel. I should be wary of her. I do not trust a soul, but trusting her would be the biggest mistake of all.

It only occurs to me now to be ashamed of how my home has fallen into disarray. I shove open one of the spare bedrooms and find it untouched, but dusty. No one has been in here for a long time. Fiora looks around her, her forehead creasing ever so slightly as she also notices that this place could use a good spring clean.

"Something wrong?" I ask defensively. Her expression softens and she shakes her head, smiling at me.

"Not at all. It has been a long time since I

spent the night in a castle," she says brightly. I fold my arms over my chest, sniffing.

"You have stayed in others? Did you trespass through those ones too?"

Fiora chuckles. "No. I grew up in a castle. The Golden Palace in Celestia. There were a thousand young witches with me, and we learned how to control our powers, how to create perfect brews, how to worship Cressida. And then we were sent off into the world and it all became a little useless."

I blink in surprise. She says it so casually that I cannot tell if she's being serious or not.

"You don't ever use your magic?"

Fiora wavers. "It depends where I go. I am a traveler, after all. I abide by the laws of wherever I go. And magic is outlawed in most places."

"It is outlawed here."

Fiora raises an eyebrow, looking amused. "That does not mean much coming from the Cursed Queen, does it? If you are willing to dabble in magic, then I think I am safe to practice it around you."

The comment makes my heart darken. I want to tell her that she has no idea what she is saying. She has no idea that I only used magic as a last resort, to save my people. For all the good it did me. Now, once again, I am forced to trust in magic to save me. The sooner Fiora helps me and gets out of here, the better.

"Take a seat on the bed. I will do my best to examine you," Fiora tells me. I glance up at the chandelier, where stubs of candles are burned down almost to the wick. It is too dark in here for her to see much.

"Shall I light the candles?"

"No need. I can handle it," Fiora says. She stands on her tiptoes and gently waves her hand over the candles. I watch as the candles flicker to life, orange flames giving the room a warm glow. It is a simple trick and yet it is still a sight to behold. Elemental magic is relatively common from what I know, but it is also strong. I get the feeling that Fiora is only giving me a small insight into what she is capable of. She gives out a satisfied sigh, admiring her handiwork.

"Well. I am glad that worked," she says with a smile. "I was worried I might be a bit rusty."

"Well that fills me with hope," I say, sitting on the dusty bedspread. I wince at my own tone. I should be more grateful that she is willing to help me. She is the first person in three years to even speak to me, and she is trying to help me out of my predicament. I guess I have forgotten how to speak to people politely.

But Fiora seems unfazed. She puts her bag on top of the wooden trunk at the foot of the bed, opening it up and digging inside.

"So, tell me more about the curse. What have you attempted in order to break it?"

"Nothing. I mean, I tried to take off my armor. I tried to go back to my ordinary life…but it has not been possible. It welded to my skin…and I was never the same again. I do not live as ordinary people do any longer."

"Do you sleep? Or eat?" Fiora asks. I shake my head slowly.

"No…the curse seems to have taken…everything. I…I do not feel much."

"Like you have been numbed?"

Hearing someone else explain what I am going through aloud makes my heart squeeze. "Yes. Exactly like that."

Fiora lets out a breath. "That is a particularly cruel curse. What caused this witch to curse you?"

"You assume it was my fault?"

"I did not say that at all," Fiora says calmly. "I only want some context."

I suck in a breath. I never realized what an irritable person I have become. I suppose there has been no one around to irk me. But Fiora is only trying to help and I keep jumping down her throat. I steady myself as I let my breath escape me once more.

"There was a battle. A terrible battle," I say quietly. "My parents led the charge against the creatures that attacked our borders. But these creatures…they were stronger than us. We are not a kingdom built to fight enemies thrice our size. And so I fled into the woods. I knew I had to do something to save my people. There is a powerful witch who lives deep in the trees. She was exiled there by my family many generations ago. She promised me invincibility for a day to take on the creatures. I battled them alone. I won the day for us all. But it came at a cost. When my time was done, my armor melded to my skin. The sensations taken from me for the battle never returned. I was left only with this scar from the end of the fight," I say, tracing my finger along the deep gash that splits my face from forehead to the left side of my face. "And my own people resent me for what I have become."

Fiora searches my face, a deep frown creasing her beautiful face. "I do not understand."

"What do you not understand?"

"You saved the lives of so many people. And they hate you for it?"

"I used magic. I did things that no human should ever be able to do. They watched me do it. And they feared me for it. They are afraid of what they do not understand."

"But if you had not done it, they would have died. All of them…"

I am shocked to see that Fiora is visibly upset by my tale. Sympathy is not something I have experienced in a long time, and it feels mildly uncomfortable. I look away, not wanting to sit in these feelings that have evaded me for so long.

"That may be so, but it does not change a thing. I just want to know if you can free me from the curse now," I say firmly. Fiora composes herself with a firm nod.

"Alright. Let me see what I can do. May I?"

I nod as she gestures to me. She steps closer to me and leans over me, sweeping my hair to one side. Her fingers brush over the skin of my neck and I shudder. The whisper of sensation that her fingers leave on me shocks me to my core. It has been far too long since I felt anything so small yet so powerful. Fiora seems to notice, her forehead creasing.

"Interesting that you felt that," she murmurs. "Perhaps it is because I have magic…it might be able to penetrate through the power of the curse."

I do not believe that has anything to do with it. It is more likely something to do with the beautiful woman touching me. But I will not say that out loud. I hold my breath as she examines the skin of my neck at the point where it meets the armor. I have stared at this very spot many times in the mirror. The transition from skin to metal is seamless. It is like the two are one and the same now.

"Fascinating," Fiora murmurs to herself. "This is certainly going to be a challenge...I may be able to brew a potion of some sort if I know more about what I am dealing with. But it will take time, and I will need to study."

"There is nothing you can do with elemental magic?"

"I do not think so. I don't believe that experimenting with it will do you any favors either. But please, give me a chance. I can always try," Fiora says earnestly. She pauses. "Did the witch give any indication at all of how the curse might be broken? For every curse, there is always a way out, even with magic as powerful as this. Did she indicate what might help you?"

I almost tell her what Laurel told me. That only the most powerful magic in the world could break this curse. But the thought of saying it aloud, of seeing Fiora's hope slip away is too much for me to bear. If I tell her that someone must love me in order to free me, then she will see just how hopeless this is. I suddenly wish I had not asked for her help at all. I stand up, pushing her aside.

"You may stay the night, but there is no need for you to uphold your end of the bargain. The situation is impossible," I insist. Fiora reaches out and touches my cheek. And there it is again. A spark of feeling, like electricity. This time, I try not to react, even though my heart is thudding impossibly hard inside my metal chest.

"I will not leave you. Not until I have attempted to help you," she says. "I will begin my work in the morning. I am going to help you get your life back. I swear it."

I want to protest, but Fiora seems as stubborn as she is sweet. I leave the room and shut the door behind me, letting the events of the evening sink in. In the space of a night, everything may have changed in a way I am completely unprepared for. All I know is that I need to keep my guard up. Fiora clearly has a power over me that I never could have anticipated. She may be working under the guise of helping me, but until I know her true intentions, I cannot allow her to get too close.

Bolt is lying in the hallway, waiting for me. She sits up and pants as I catch her eye, looking pleased with herself. I fix her a look.

"Do not get attached," I warn her.

The sooner Fiora leaves, the better.

Chapter Four

I do not see much of Fiora and her companions for a few days. The castle is large, and the four of them seem intent on exploring every nook and cranny. I caught Calla and Sigrid trying to peek in the library last night when I was reading and I was forced to shoo them away. While Fiora has some use here, the others are simply a nuisance. Still, so long as they keep to themselves, I will tolerate them. In some ways, it makes this castle feel more alive, like they are breathing life into it. I cannot deny that now that I have had time to settle, it feels good to hear voices around here that are not just the echoes of my thoughts.

I try to go about my days as usual. Bolt and I head out into the woods to chop wood. The merchant from town comes to collect it, as he does every Friday, and I silently hand over the goods to him. I spend my nights in the library, opting not to join my guests in the dining hall while they eat and joke and converse. I do not see the sense in being around them. For one thing, Neville seems terrified of me, Sigrid eyes me up with cruel disapproval, and Calla gets nervous giggles whenever I am around. As for Fiora, she is here with a purpose that does not involve friendship. They are only staying here until Fiora's bargain is fulfilled and Calla's ankle heals. Then I will be left here alone again.

But now and then, I dare to dream about how things will be if Fiora manages to break the curse. Once I shed my armor, will my people see me as one of them again? Will they forgive my missteps and accept me as their queen? Will I finally be able to rule as I should instead of them living in fear of me?

It is still not the life I envisioned for myself. I never pictured myself on a throne. I dreamed of love and travel and adventure once, like the stories in the books I read. I knew that someday my duties would force me to serve my kingdom, but I imagined that I would at least have time before then. That perhaps I would have time to find a wife from a far away kingdom, someone willing to join our kingdoms together in marriage so we could rule side by side. And maybe once we settled, we could adopt a child and have a new adventure.

But those dreams shattered three years ago,

and the glass shards of those fanciful wishes still dig in my feet as I walk to my future. I walk this path alone.

Unless Fiora can help me.

She has been here for four days now, and I am beginning to grow restless. I want to see how she is progressing. After I hear the others return to their quarters for the evening, I knock at Fiora's door, keen to find out if she is getting anywhere.

When she opens the door, I try not to be rendered breathless by how she looks. She is wearing a golden nightgown made of fine silk, miles of her skin on show in the moonlight. The swirls of her tattoos travel over her limbs, intricate patterns that make me want to stare at her for hours to decipher them. I try to focus on her face, though it is equally enchanting in a way that easily knocks my guard down. She looks tired, but she smiles anyway, as though she might be glad to see me. The impossibility of that idea grounds me. This is simply a woman trying to fulfill a promise.

"Alana…I was not expecting to see you at this hour. In fact, I have not seen you much at all since my arrival."

"I keep myself busy," I say gruffly. I do not want to stand here and make small talk. Not when every minute in her presence is like torture to me, pushing unwanted feelings right to the surface. After so long of feeling numb, it is a struggle to cope with these emotions hounding me. "I was hoping you might have made some progress."

"Alana…I told you that this would take time. I am doing the best I can. But come in, sit with me a while. Perhaps I can explain to you what I have been working on."

She steps aside to allow me into her room. It is cleaner than when I last came in here, but there is mess everywhere I look. There are piles of books stacked against the four poster bed, and I can smell something earthy brewing in a pot by the open window. Sheets of paper are arranged across the floor, and there is a cushion where Fiora has clearly been sitting. She opens her arms to show me the chaos.

"There is a method to the madness, I promise you," she says, her lips forming a smile. "I have been scouring every book I own…"

"Where did all of these come from?" I ask, staring around in astonishment. "You arrived with only one bag…"

"Magic, dearest, can do things beyond your wildest imaginings," Fiora says mischievously. She pauses. "But still, it has its limitations. As you know, elemental magic is my specialty. There is little I cannot achieve with fire, water, earth, wind…but breaking this curse is beyond those abilities. So the potion I am brewing…it is an attempt to try other types of magic. I am still learning how to brew…but my tutor believes I will go on to do great things."

I sigh. "Doing great things is not something to strive for. It only brings you trouble."

Fiora's eyes soften. "What you did for your people was the most selfless thing I have ever heard of, Alana. That is something to be proud of."

"It is hard to feel pride when everyone else wants me to feel shame," I snap. Alana threads her fingers together, refusing to look away from me.

"I do not want you to be ashamed. And I also do not want you to lose sight of the good in your heart. The good that drove you to save all of those people in the first place."

"What would you know about the goodness of my heart, witch?" I snarl. In moments like this, I can feel myself getting out of control, but I cannot seem to help it. Years of bitterness have made me angrier than I can ever remember being before. "You do not know me. Do not presume to tell me who I am."

"Only a good person would do what you did," Fiora says firmly. "You may not believe it yourself, but it is true. You could have run away and spared yourself. You sacrificed everything. Those are not the actions of a selfish person. And believe me, I have met plenty of bad people on my travels. You are angry, hurt, aggressive at times…but you are good at heart. I know it."

I am left breathless by her comments. I can feel the hot rage inside me dulling down again, making me embarrassed for the way I spoke to her. I run a hand through my hair.

"I…I am sorry. I should never have spoken to you that way."

"That's okay," Fiora says mildly, unfazed. "Although I do prefer to be called by name, not simply *witch*. I understand the anger you harbor toward my kind…given what happened to you. But I assure you that I am only trying to help. And though magic is seen as villainous, I believe that is only true when it falls in the wrong hands."

"I know. I am truly sorry. I have no idea what is coming over me…"

Fiora steps toward me and places her hand on my arm. I cannot feel her touch here through the metal of my armor, but it sends a jolt through me regardless. I look at her hand, her fingers delicately placed out of the way of the thorns protruding from the armor. She is the only person who has tried to touch me in three years. She does not appear fazed by how sharp the spikes are, how easily they could slice through her delicate skin.

"You must be lonely here after so many years," she whispers, her dark eyes meeting mine. There is an empathy so deep in those eyes that it makes me ache. "If I was you, I would be exactly the same. I have taken a more fortunate path in life, but I have met many people on my travels who have been less lucky. So allow me to ease your worries. You are doing the best you can with the hand you have been dealt. It is not the end of the line. Things can get better. I swear it to you."

It is hard to break away from her gaze, so I don't. For the first time since her arrival, I allow myself to feel the stirrings she has coaxed out of me. It is foreign, but not as unwelcome as I expected it to be now. I let out a quiet sigh.

"You have a way with words...has anybody ever told you that?"

Fiora laughs. "Several times."

"Is it a form of magic?"

She smiles. "Perhaps. But you do not need to be a witch to possess it."

"You say that, and yet I always say the wrong thing. How very human of me."

Fiora smiles and moves her hand to cup my face. I cannot get used to the way she uses touch. So many years of no contact make her affectionate ways even more intense. It takes everything in me not to sigh against her touch, to lean my face into her palm.

"Humanity is no bad thing," she says gently. When her hand moves from my cheek, I miss it right away. She turns her back on me and examines her workings. "But patience is something that you could perhaps try mastering. You cannot expect magic like this to work overnight, as much as you might want it to."

I sigh. "My apologies. Your hard work is appreciated."

"I am glad to hear it. I will keep trying. But there is no need for you to be a stranger. You can come to me whenever you wish. Though I do tend to try and sleep at this hour."

"I will leave you be," I say, bowing out of the room. As I close the door once again, I realize that I stepped into the room feeling like one person and left feeling like another. What is it about her? Does she breathe the kind of magic that soothes those around her?

Or am I simply just forgetting what it is like to be in the company of someone kind?

Chapter Five

Six days pass again without much change, aside from my efforts to be a little more welcoming to my guests. I invite them all to pet Bolt when we pass them in the corridors, and I ask them polite questions that can be answered quickly enough for me to escape the conversation whenever I like.

Calla is pleasant to me most of all, and Sigrid seems to warm to me a little, asking me questions about my weapons and my training. Neville tends to keep his distance, and I cannot blame him after the welcome I gave him the night he arrived. Still, I have no true incentive to be anything beyond polite. They will be gone soon enough, and they will be just fine without my presence.

But curiosity about Fiora convinces me to make a little effort, at least. Tonight, I decide to join them all for dinner, though I do not eat or even speak much. I listen to the others throwing around jokes, telling lewd stories and wishing that I had some part in them. At least Fiora smiles at me from time to time, making me feel like I am a part of it all rather than an outsider. That much I can appreciate.

I can tell it puts Neville on edge to be around me, so after the others have finished up their plates, I retire to the library once again, running over the interactions at dinner a thousand times in my mind and torturing myself over my awkwardness. There is little that can convince me that it went well. All I can picture is them whispering about me as I left them there; the strange Cursed Queen who does not know how to hold an ordinary conversation.

I hide my head in a book and try to distract myself from it all. But it is the middle of the night when I hear a squeal from somewhere down the hallway. My thoughts immediately go to Fiora and I quickly vacate the library, rushing to see if she is alright. As I run down the hallway, I can see smoke snaking beneath the door to her bedroom. My heart freezes. What on earth has she managed to do?

I throw the door open and find Fiora on her knees beside the window. The potion in her cauldron seems to be overflowing and she is grimacing in pain, clutching her wrist. There is an angry red mark on her skin, blistering and bubbling on the surface.

"Fiora," I breathe. She looks up at me with a pained expression, but all the while, she is waving me off.

"I am well, do not worry. It is just a small burn."

"It does not look small to me. Here, allow me to help you…"

She doesn't protest as I rush to examine the damage. She lets out a small chuckle, shaking her head to herself.

"The potion is not going well, I confess," she tells me, chewing her lip. "I hate to admit my shortcomings…but potion craft has never been easy for me."

"Never mind that now. Have you got something to treat the wound?" I ask. "Some ointment, perhaps?"

"Fortunately, yes. This is certainly not the first time I have got myself into trouble. If you take a look on top of the trunk, there is a mortar with a paste I prepared for this exact scenario. At least I came prepared, right?"

I am barely listening to her babble as I find the mortar containing an aromatic green paste. The smell takes me back. My mother prepared something similar to this many times when I was a child. I was always getting myself into trouble, injuring myself in training or touching poisonous plants or getting too close to the fire. I can recall the crackling of flames on my own skin, and I wince at the memory. I forgot how being in Fiora's presence seems to amplify feelings, new and old. I push them aside and return to her, examining her arm. It looks terribly sore, but her expression remains level.

"Are you alright?" I ask tenderly. It is almost a shock to hear the concern in my own voice. It has been a while since I spoke in such soft tones. Fiora chuckles again.

"Yes, I will be fine. I tend to believe we as women learn to tolerate various aches and pains. It is not like we are strangers to bleeding, is it? Each month when thorns wrap around my insides, I remind myself that I survive it every time. I am old enough now to know that womanhood is pain."

"I can barely recall how it feels," I admit quietly. "I haven't bled since I received the curse."

"Oh, Alana…I am so sorry."

I chuckle. "There is no need to be. I have no use for it. It is one of the few blessings of this curse. Not to be in pain every month."

"I can see how that would appeal," she says with a gentle smile. I hold up the mortar to her.

"Do I just apply it to the burn?"

"There is no need for you to stay…I can do

this myself."

"Nonsense," I wave her off. "You got hurt trying to assist me. I will not leave you now."

Fiora's lips quirk into a smile. "Yes, ma'am. In that case, yes. Gentle as you can."

Gentle has never particularly suited me. I have always been the kind of person who barrels through life, leaving a path of destruction behind me. But now, I scoop some of the paste onto my fingers and tentatively brush it across Fiora's skin. She winces ever so slightly, but she doesn't make a fuss. As my fingers move across her broken skin, a strange feeling overcomes me. I realize that this is the first time I have willingly touched someone in a very long time. Fiora may have initiated contact a number of times since she arrived, but now that I am returning the gesture, it feels so odd. I look up and find that she is watching me. Heat rushes into my cheeks.

"Is this okay?"

"It is," she says, her eyes not leaving mine. It makes my chest tighten. I break her gaze and continue to spread the paste onto her arm as gently as I can.

"I was just thinking about my mother," I blurt out. "She used to use something like this on my skin when I was a child. The smell…it reminded me of her."

"You must miss her terribly."

The room suddenly feels far too hot. What am I doing, telling her these things as though we are old friends? She has no interest in my past. I say nothing more, continuing to tend to her arm. Fiora seems to sense that I am not keen to continue the conversation because she changes its course. She sighs.

"The potion has failed. I expected that it would...but it is disheartening all the same," she says. "I believe I have exhausted my options from the books I have. I will have to think about how to proceed."

I turn to look at the still bubbling cauldron. Smoke billows out of the window and into the night. I should be more concerned about the failed attempt. If a powerful witch cannot help me now, then perhaps I am beyond help.

But perhaps there is something I can do to help. After all, I have a library filled wall to wall with books. I have kept it off limits to my guests so far. I do not want them snooping around in there, invading the one space that feels like it belongs to me.

But Fiora is here to help me, and she is nothing like her companions. Where they feel loud and abrasive and nosy, she is serene and calm like a spring morning. If there is anyone in this world left that I can trust with my sacred space, perhaps it is her.

"Would you like to see the library?" I ask her. Surprise flickers across her face.

"Are you inviting me to look?"

"Purely for the purpose of your work," I say a little defensively, though I am not sure I mean it. I imagine if anyone in this world would appreciate the library, it is her. I also feel that some part of me is keen to impress her. "My parents may not have agreed with magic, but my father in particular had an interest in potions. I imagine there are some books in there that will suit your purposes."

"Then I would be glad to take a look," Fiora says. "Just let me clean up here a little…"

I watch as she holds out her good arm and angles her hand toward the fire beneath the cauldron. A sudden jet of water shoots forward and douses the flames, allowing the bubbling potion to recede to the base of the cauldron. Fiora catches my eye with a sparkle in her gaze.

Perhaps I am not the only one trying to impress here.

"You can follow me," I tell Fiora. I stand, brushing away the remnants of the ointment on my hands and head in the direction of the library.

Fiora falls in step beside me, her tall frame almost level with my own. It feels strange to walk next to a woman who is similar to me in stature and to consider her so beautiful. I have always felt too big for this world with broad shoulders, a soft stomach, muscled arms. My height has always been a source of insecurity too. Everyone has some part of them that desires beauty, craves it deeply, because it determines our place in the world, no matter how we wish it wouldn't. Even as a child, I declined to wear dresses, preferring not to allow anybody to see the body I felt so shunned for. I loved the idea of wearing something so beautiful, and yet I never felt that I deserved to.

But I see Fiora and I feel differently. I see features in her that match my own, and yet it is as though she wears it better. How can we be the same and yet so different? Is it my eyes deceiving me when I look in the mirror, warping myself into the monster that my people have declared me to be? Is it possible that from the outside, someone may see me the way I see Fiora?

It feels impossible. I have grown so hateful toward myself that it feels like I might never recover from it. The curse was a catalyst, but it wasn't the beginning. I have always tried to hide myself away. Now that I am trapped behind my armor, I have other things to worry about. But some part of me hopes that Fiora sees me through kinder eyes. That perhaps she sees the beauty I have craved for so long.

I have to force myself to shake myself internally. Now is not the time to start beating myself up again. I am finally getting somewhere with Fiora. I must not taint this interaction with my negativity. As we reach the library, I try to push thoughts of self-deprecation to the back of my mind. Fiora looks at me expectantly and my hand hovers over the brass door handle, hesitant for a short moment. I have come too far to turn her away now. I take a breath and push it open.

The library is the kind of place that invites awe into my heart, even after living in this castle all my life. I watch Fiora's face light up as she sees how many books this room holds in its embrace. The smell of paper and candle wax gives this room a warm feeling. In the past few years, this is the only place where I have felt truly alive. A thousand lives are trapped inside the pages of these books, just waiting to be discovered.

"It has been a long time since I last saw a library this grand," Fiora breathes. "Back in Celestia, there was a large library where we were sent to study…but this one is much more beautiful."

"It is blessed by our goddess, Selene," I tell

her. "I am sure your goddess enhanced your lands in ways of her own…but here, everything we do and the ways we live are inspired by nature. She offered up the wood from her trees to forge these bookcases, to make so many books. That is why libraries seem so magical. They are touched by Selene's blessings. We torture our world in many ways…we cut down the trees she makes, clear her fields to make houses, crack open the rocks she provides for ore…but libraries are a blessing that no one could deny. A true appreciation of her offerings."

"I may not worship your goddess, but I wholeheartedly agree," Fiora says, her lips parted as she looks around her. Then her eyes fall upon me. "Do you like to read?"

I take a deep breath, my heart lifting at the question. "I love to read. More than almost anything else these days."

Fiora smiles. "Me too. Staying on the road traveling does not make it easy to read, though. It is hard to look where you are going when your head is stuck in a book. "

I surprise us both by laughing a little. I see Fiora's expression flicker between shock and then joy. My laugh is gravelly and loud - not becoming in the slightest - but it has been so long since I heard it that it feels good to indulge in it. Fiora laughs a little too, a faint blush appearing on her cheeks.

"Do you mind if I take a look around?" she asks after a moment. "I promise I will leave as soon as I have found what I am looking for. I understand that this space is important to you. I know you spend your evenings here."

I waver. Now that Fiora is in here, it doesn't feel so daunting. Would it be so bad to allow her to stay here? To listen to her shuffling around barefoot, gently prying dusty books from their homes on the shelves? Would it be so bad to share my love of books with someone else? I thought when she first arrived that she would be a nuisance, constantly standing in my way. Now, I am beginning to think that perhaps some company would be nice.

"You do not have to leave," I say gently. "You can stay here, read in one of the comfy chairs…let your room air out from your disastrous potion…"

Fiora laughs. "Well, I do not believe I can say no to that. Alright, I will stay. But if I am disturbing you, feel free to shoo me away. I do not want to be bothersome."

You could never be, I think before I can stop myself. My stomach twists. I need to give myself a good shake. Fiora is only here to save the skins of her trespassing friends and to help me.

She is *not* here to make friends. And after the way I have treated her, she certainly will not be interested in being friends with *me*. I harden my expression.

"So long as you keep the noise down, I am sure we can co-exist here just fine," I say gruffly. Fiora does not look fazed by my coldness at all. She simply places a finger to her lips with a warm smile.

"Of course. We are in a library after all."

I cannot help the smile that tugs on my lips. It is only now that I am realizing how dangerous this woman is to me. I may have wrapped myself in thorns, but she seems intent on untangling me from them, no matter how many times she may prick her fingers. Maybe she believes that somewhere deep down, if she looks hard enough, she will find a heart still as soft as a rose petal.

And I want to believe she is right.

Chapter Six

It is late by the time Fiora leaves the library. I have lost myself in a book, but the moment she touches my cheek to let me know she is going, I return immediately to the present. In the book I am reading, two lovers just touched for the first time. My own feelings seem to echo the words still swimming around my mind.

"I will retire for the night," she tells me gently. "Goodnight. I will pick up where I left off in the morning."

"Sleep well," I murmur. I should thank her for all that she is doing for me, but further words catch in my throat. Why is it so difficult to find the words I need when she is close to me?

She leaves, her nightgown sweeping behind her gracefully. The beauty and elegance of her stay on my mind as I try to return to reading. I cannot concentrate on the book any longer, so I decide that a walk might help calm my racing thoughts. It is nights like these, when restlessness is even more rife than usual, that I climb up to the highest point in the castle, dizzying myself as I navigate winding stairs to the raven tower.

I reach the top, the small circular room flooded with the gentle light of the moon. It smells pretty terrible up here considering that this is where the ravens roost, but you cannot beat the view.

I stand by the window and observe my kingdom. From up here, I can see the great vine walls that snake around our lands, keeping us safe. I see how they stretch beyond the small town where my people live and beyond into the dense forest. Of all of the kingdoms in the land, mine is one of the smaller ones. We only have a small population, a tiny town that is made up of a close knit community. It is no wonder they refuse to forgive and forget those who have slighted them. I think that is why they hold on to their hatred for me. It is better to hate the monarch on the hill than their neighbors.

The families in Thornwood have been here for generations. Some marry into other kingdoms, but many stay here their whole lives. I never imagined that I would be one of them. Somehow, even though my destiny has always been entwined with Thornwood, it always felt like somewhere to reside until the rest of the world offered itself up to me.

I can see everything that I have ever known within my eyeline. Even the few neighboring kingdoms that I have visited are just within reach, shrouded now by the fog that settles constantly over the land. I think of all of the places Fiora must have visited on her travels, the incredible things she must've seen. And then she came here, to this small kingdom with so little to offer. Does she pity me, for being stuck here?

All of a sudden, it is as though the vine walls are closing around my throat, suffocating me in this place. I have not left the kingdom in years. I have barely even stepped out beyond the castle grounds. I am trapped in the kingdom by duty, and shunted away from the town by my own people.

It occurs to me sometimes that there is more to my kingdom than what lies at the base of the hill. Beyond the town, deep in the woods, there is so much I know nothing about. Laurel proved that to me. I wonder about her sometimes, wondering if she still resides there in her horrible cottage. She wanted me to change life for her during my reign, but I never once considered going to meet with her again. Not after what she was willing to do with me. It became clear to me in the aftermath why she was exiled in the first place.

It only reminds me that I should be careful of Fiora. She is a witch, after all. Magic has brought nothing but trouble my way. She might be enchanting, she may make me feel things that I should not feel, but all the more reason to avoid her.

Falling for her is the most dangerous thing I could ever do.

I hear the flap of wings outside the window and look up to see a raven returning with a piece of paper in its beak. I frown. In the middle of the night? What is the meaning of this?

The note written on the paper is in frantic scrawl, almost unreadable. I hold my breath as I scan over the words.

Your majesty,

Trouble has returned to our borders. The creatures have returned for vengeance. Please help us.

My heart jolts and I glance out of the window once again. Now, I can see fires lit in the far distance, villagers holding torches as they watch the problem rolling in.

I never thought I would have to see those

awful creatures again, but here they are once again. I can see their ominous shadows looming close to the walls, scuttling closer to the town.

My heart tugs in my chest. I am both scared and angry. Scared that these things have come to call again, and that this time I will be unprotected. Angry that these people who have shunned me for so long now expect me to save them once again. They do not care how much of a risk it will be for me, or that I will likely die on the battlefield. They only want to save themselves again and then shoo me back up to my castle until they need me next.

But I am not so bitter and twisted that I will abandon them in their hour of need. It is my duty to protect them.

I will not fail them, no matter how many times they fail me in return.

I hurtle down the stairs, calling out for Bolt. I shall need her for the battle ahead. I cannot do this alone. Fear grips my heart at the thought of something happening to her, but she will not perceive the danger. She is stronger than I give her credit for. She will be an asset to me out there.

She comes running to me as I call her, but she is not the only one. Fiora comes out of her room, her arms crossed over her chest. Down the hallway, Calla and Sigrid emerge too, looking concerned.

"What is going on?" Fiora asks. I turn to her briefly.

"Trouble has come to my town. I must see to it," I tell her.

"Then I will come with you."

"Nonsense. Go back to bed."

"I will not. I am trained for battle too, you know," Fiora insists. She nods to Sigrid. "And Sigrid too. Her music has been known to influence a battle."

"She is not a witch…how is that possible?"

"She plays a magical lute that we secured on our travels. It has got us out of a fair few scrapes."

Sigrid nods. "I can lead your enemy a merry dance. And if that fails, I am handy with a knife."

"Even if the enemy is a mile high arachnid creature, not a human?"

Sigrid shrugs. "It is strong magic I wield. And my knife is very sharp."

I want to tell them both to stay where they are, but I know that I cannot do this alone. If I do not return, the castle will eventually be overwhelmed anyway. Their survival relies on me as much as mine may rely on theirs. I need all of the help they are willing to offer.

"Okay. We must hurry," I tell them. Calla

presses a fleeting kiss to Sigrid's lips.

"Be safe. I will prepare the horses while you armor up."

"There is no time to waste," I insist, already rushing down the stairs. "Every second we wait, someone may die. That is something I cannot allow."

Chapter Seven

The three of us ride down the hill into the town, me riding on Bolt's back, Fiora and Sigrid on their horses. If the situation was not so dire, I might stop to admire just how stunning Fiora looks in her armor. Her gold breastplate and mail skirting bulk out her slim frame, making her look as powerful as she is on the inside. For the first time in years, I have had to don armor of my own aside from the breastplate that remains as much a part of me as my own skin. It is heavy on my body as we ride to the battle. I know right away that this is going to be more dangerous than the first time around, but also much more difficult. I will have to battle with my armor weighing me down, with the knowledge that one stray pincer could slice through me and end my life. It is far from a comforting thought.

I can hear the screams of the villagers now as we ride through the town. Many of my people are running into their houses with no desire to face what exists beyond the borders. I cannot blame them. The last thing I would like to do is fight a losing battle. This is how my parents must have felt, headed toward the battle knowing they likely wouldn't survive it. I ready my double headed battle axe, swinging it once in preparation. I left my sword behind, feeling that I needed something stronger for this battle. At least I have had plenty of time to train up, to ready myself to battle once again. I have no desire to fight unprepared ever again. But will it be enough to save me? I feel certain of absolutely nothing.

Now, the creatures come into view over the wall, their claw-like bodies scurrying too close to the borders. We need to stop them before they climb the vines or manage to make it through the main gate.

"Open the gate!" I cry to the villages who are standing close to it uselessly, trying to figure out what to do. They do as they are told, hauling the wooden doors open to allow the three of us through.

No one attempts to follow us.

I take one last glance at Fiora. I want something to hold onto for this battle. Something beautiful to guide me through the ugliness. Then, with a battle cry of rage, I plow my way into the fray.

Fear scuttles across my skin. No curse can numb how terrifying this is. The creatures seem taller than they did the first time. Maybe they simply terrify me more now that I do not have anything but my armor to protect me. Still, there are much fewer of them this time. I can see a few dozen in my eyeline, nothing like the onslaught three years ago. It is almost like they scrounged together their leftovers to fight us. Hope rises inside me. Perhaps this is a battle we can win after all.

Fiora and Sigrid split off without a word, seeming to know what they are doing. Bolt growls as we are left alone, but she knows where to go. She heads to the flanks of the arachnid army and snaps at the legs of one of the creatures. The monster makes a hissing noise that sends a shiver down my spine, dancing out of the way of Bolt's snapping jaw. I feel far too small against this thing. I need to go for the legs, cripple it and stop it from getting any closer to crossing my borders. With all the strength I can muster, I swing my axe.

It hits home on the creature's leg, but it is like a pebble hitting a boulder. It does nothing. There is no sign of even a dent in its armoring. How can that be? I know how much force I put into that hit. The creature should be felled now.

I blink, preparing to swing again. I duck away from a swipe from the towering creature, ready to try another method of attack. If the legs are a no go, and the belly is too risky, then I need to go higher.

I tug on Bolt's fur and direct her toward the vine wall. She puts her trust in me, running from the creature. When we are close enough to the wall, I jump from my saddle and grapple on to one of the thick vines threading through to create the wall. My heavy armor slows me down, but I begin to climb up, to get some height. If I can lure the creature in, I should be at the right height now to go for the eyes. It is the only other weak spot that I can think of.

Sure enough, the creature pursues me to the wall. These things had few brains the first time around, and it seems nothing has changed. It gets close enough that its eyes are level with my body. It should be easy to swing and blind it, so I do. My axe makes a swift arc, hitting the monster square in the eyes.

But to my horror, my axe comes back clean. Once again, the creature has somehow blocked my attacks. It is almost as though my axe is blunt.

Something is wrong. Very wrong. These things were never easy to kill, but they never used to be this strong, this impenetrable. I think of the soft underbelly, my final hope, but before I can try and form a plan, a huge pincer slices across my face.

Before I can react, I am tumbling from the wall, hot pain blinding me momentarily. My body hits the ground hard and I roll over, winded and bruised. I try to scramble to my feet, but the pain sends me flat on my back again. I try to blink it away, try to see through it, but it is not going away. I can feel blood on my skin and my cheekbone feels as though it's splintered. It seems that pain this bad can surpass my curse. I can feel it all, the sensation loud and clear.

Bolt howls, running to my aid. Her teeth clank on the metal of my armor as she tries to pull me away by my shoulder, away from the battle, but I am still dizzied, trying to figure out what happened. Why are they so much stronger now? Why can I not seem to harm them like I could before? My eyes fall closed as I try to navigate the pain. I know I need to get to my feet, to fight, to defend myself. If I fail to, I will surely die.

I prise my eyes open as Bolt pulls at me. The creature does not appear to be pursuing me. Perhaps it believes I died from the fall. I am lucky I didn't. At least nothing appears to be broken. For once I am glad of my metal torso. I blink several times, trying to bring the world back into focus.

Across the land, I can see fire. Not like the torches of the villagers, but great walls of it, unnatural amounts spreading through the air.

And then behind it is Fiora. Her arms are raised to the sky atop her horse, raining hell down as she summons the fire of a thousand suns on the creatures.

And I can see that they are falling hard and fast. They screech wildly as the fire consumes them, shriveling away the plates of their outer shells. It is horrifying, but necessary. Without Fiora's fire, I would likely be dead already.

And then I hear the haunting music drifting from the borders. It must be Sigird on her lute. She has climbed up the vine wall and is teasing a somber tune from the instrument. I watch as the creatures become transfixed by it, swaying on the spot to the sound of the tune.

Right up until the moment that Fiora shifts her wall of fire and burns them alive.

I try to get to my feet to help them, though it is quickly becoming clear to me that they are of much more use here than I am. Bolt whines as I manage to plant my feet on the ground, despite the dizziness taking over me. I try to pick up my axe, but it is far too heavy right now to keep me balanced. I fall to one knee again, defeated. I can only watch as Sigrid and Fiora take center stage, Sigrid luring in the creatures with her song before Fiora burns them to a crisp.

It must be magic. That is the only conclusion I can come to for why these creatures are so hard to destroy now. The same sort of magic that stopped me from dying three years ago on the battlefield has returned with a new host. But Fiora is proving that they can be stopped. *Magic knows magic,* she told me not so long ago. And now, it seems it is our only hope.

I watch the creatures lose the battle. I watch until every single one of them has fallen, until the grass beneath me is scorched with fire. Only then does Fiora shakily lower her hands, the fire flickering away as though it was never there to begin with. Sigrid's song comes to an end, and the night is left in an engulfing silence.

Bolt soon begins to whine, anxious to know if I am okay. I pet her head absently, thrown off by everything I have just seen. I will be left with bruises and cuts, but the thing that really makes an impression on me is the fear this has brought to me. If Fiora and Sigrid weren't here, we would have been doomed. We are powerless against such powerful magic. I can see now why my parents feared it so much, why they did everything to suppress it and hide it away. If magic was allowed to rule, life would never be the same again.

I stagger to greet Fiora and Sigrid. They too look shaken by the battle. Fiora hops down from her horse, her boots crunching on the scorched earth. She touches my good cheek, examining the place where the pincer sliced me open. My face has been torn open so many times now that scars top older scars.

"I can treat this," she murmurs. Her eyes meet mine. "Are you alright? I…I saw you fall. I wanted to come to you…"

"I will live," I say gruffly. We have bigger concerns than my battered body. "We need to get back to the castle quickly. The townsfolk will not take kindly to what they just saw."

Sigrid's forehead creases in irritation. "We just saved their lives."

"That will not matter to them. I saved them three years ago and they turned against me. They never forgave the magic I used. You will not be safe if you stay around here."

Fiora looks anxious, but she nods in understanding. She knows more of what I have endured than Sigrid does. She understands the need to hightail out of here. "Alright. We can speak more at the castle."

I mount Bolt again with some difficulty, my body throbbing with pain, but I have no intention of sticking around to see what the villagers are willing to do to us. It would be a cruel ending to survive such a hard battle only to be skewered by the pitchforks of an angry mob.

As we ride through the town, exhausted from the short, but intense battle, the townsfolk are gathering in the streets, whispering among themselves. I spy familiar faces from the last time I went to battle, their expressions unchanged. They have not become any more forgiving with time. And now, I am riding by with a witch and a woman with an enchanted lute. They are not going to take kindly to my return.

"Witch!" a man cries from the crowd. And that is when I see him launch a stone at Fiora. It hits her back and she gasps, perhaps more in shock than in pain, but anger flares inside me, hot and wild. I tug Bolt to a halt and dismount, storming over to the man and grabbing him by the scruff of his shirt.

"What is wrong with you?" I snarl. "This woman just saved your life."

"We never asked for your help!" the man spits back.

"Someone among you did! I received a raven begging for my assistance. And I came out of the goodness of my heart. But perhaps next time I will leave you all to die. Ungrateful beasts!"

I have not felt anger like this in so long. I am used to their stone cold hatred for me, but to see them turn on Fiora too…it is too much. I know I should keep my cool. I should walk away. But I feel this fierce need to protect her from everything I have endured. To protect her full stop.

The one thing that brings me back to earth is the look on the faces of the other villagers. There is pure, unadulterated fear in their eyes. They have never stopped seeing me as a monster. And now, with the swell of anger inside me, I feel like one.

But there is no winning with these people, so blinded by terror and hate. There is nothing I can do for them, no way to talk sense into them. I have to leave before this truly gets ugly.

I let the man go. I sniff, stepping back.

"I have stayed out of your way. I have exiled myself and allowed you all to live unburdened by me. Perhaps you can at least extend some courtesy by not attacking me and my friends each time we come to your aid," I say darkly. Then, before they can toss any more stones, I return to Bolt and she takes me away, Sigrid and Fiora following close behind. I am trembling with hurt and fury. How has it come to this? Where did I go so wrong?

I cling to Bolt and try not to allow tears to fall from my eyes. I must maintain my composure. I must not show my hurt.

Monsters do not cry.

Chapter Eight

We arrive back at the castle to find Calla and Neville waiting by the gate anxiously. When Calla catches sight of Sigrid arriving on her horse, she covers her mouth to suppress a sob, running to her wife and helping her down from her horse. There, they embrace tightly, and it makes me feel as though they are squeezing my throat, not each other. My mood has turned particularly foul, and the last thing I need is to be reminded that there is no one to meet me after battle. No one is glad to see me alive, no one is here to hold me and tell me that it will all be okay now. It only reminds me how bitter I truly am. Their show of affection has nothing to do with me, and yet I seem to turn it into a personal attack.

While Neville and Fiora talk in low voices, I stalk back up to the castle, my body hurting and my heart squeezing. I want to go somewhere where I can be alone and not have to appear as the wounded animal that I feel I am right now.

It has been a long time since I spent time in my old bedroom, but that is where I head now. I need to lie down. I may not need to sleep or eat, but for the first time in a long time, my body is alive with feeling, and the main one is exhaustion. I suppose I will just have to lay down and wait for the feeling to go away and for my body to recharge.

I try to keep my mind devoid of thought, to stray my mind from the horrific battle and the cruel townsfolk, but it is not easy. I can remember as a child that sleep was the cure for every ailment, for every bad day I had and every day I wanted to disappear, but I do not have that luxury anymore. I remain trapped with my own mind, every hour of every day. I have to sit with the knowledge that I am unloved no matter how I try to win over the favor of my peers. I curl into myself. It hurts more than my open wound, my battered body. Those things will go away at some point. But I will live my life alone and there is nothing I can do to prevent it.

It feels like hours pass before I hear a knock on the door. It opens without me answering, and I see Fiora standing in the doorway, supplies gathered in a small basket.

"I have been looking for you for some

time…you disappeared. I had to check every room in the castle…"

"What do you want?" I ask. I know I am being rude to her when I have no reason to be, but my anger feels like it has to point somewhere. She ignores my tone.

"I said I would tend to your wounds. It is the least I can do."

"I do not need your help."

"Nonsense. Sit up and I will make sure that your wound doesn't get infected."

"Why should you care what happens to me?"

Fiora doesn't take the bait. She kneels down beside my bed, sorting through her supplies, and so I eventually sit up silently, waiting for her to say something more.

"I never thanked you for how you stood up for me. Back in the town."

I sniff. "For all the good it did us."

"I know what is bothering you. I know how it must hurt to have them treat you this way. And I cannot tell you simply to forget it, because I know that is not the nature of letting things go. But you are worth more than they make you feel. I wish that you could see that."

I scoff. "All I see is what I have become. I feel as though I left my true self in the past long ago. I am so…so full of anger and hate. I never wanted to be this way. But I cannot change it now. It is in my blood. It is a part of the curse."

Fiora's face softens. "Did the witch tell you that or is that simply what you believe? You have every right to be mad at the world, Alana. Perhaps it is not the curse…just a natural response to the cruelty you have endured. But it is not too late. You do not need to give in to it."

"That is easy for you to say. Whenever you come across an issue, you can just walk away from it. If not for your obligations to me, you would have left this kingdom the moment that stone hit your back. But I am trapped here alone. I have had days like today every day for three years. There is no relief. It does not matter whether the curse is what makes me so hateful. I am what I am. And how can I change that when I know that no one can ever truly care for me, no matter what I do?"

"Another story you tell yourself, dearest. Who says that nobody cares for you?"

I throw my hands up in frustration. "I do! Because I have no one! I do not have a single person in my life who has stuck around. That is how I know."

"Alana…do you think I would have rode into battle for someone I do not care about? Do you think I would have wasted my time searching for you to tend to your wounds if I did not care? You matter. You matter to me."

I blink in shock. It has been so long since I heard somebody say that to me, and now Fiora is just tossing out important words as though they cost her nothing. It feels impossible to comprehend. I have lashed out at her, I have treated her cruelly, I have refused to repay her kindnesses. What could possibly make her care for me?

She begins to clean the wound on my face calmly, a rag wiping blood from my skin. It stings a little, but I am transfixed by Fiora and her words. She makes it sound so simple - that I matter even if nobody has ever made me feel as though I do. I sit quietly with my thoughts as she patches me up. She has this way of making me see things from a new viewpoint, no matter how much I might not want to. She sees light where I only see darkness. She is the star lighting my blackest night.

I do not want to feel this way, to have so much reliance on a person to shape my moods. But the longer I spend with her, I realize that she is the reason I fought today. The reason I will not give up. The reason that some part of me, deep down, still sees a way out of the dark.

She finishes her work, her tender fingers brushing my cheek. Our eyes latch on, her face too close to mine.

It takes my breath away. Feeling rushes

through my body, feeling that I have not had in so long. Craving. Need. Desire. I look at Fiora and it lights a fire inside me. I want to reach out and touch her skin. I want to hold her body against mine. I want to kiss her, to get lost in her so I can pretend she and I are the only things that exist.

She exhales and I get this funny feeling that her thoughts might mirror my own. She hesitates, moving just a little closer to me. Close enough that I could tilt my head upwards and our lips would touch. It would be so easy to do.

I turn my head to the side.

I cannot place the reason I did it. Perhaps some part of me knows that I am not good enough for her. That no matter my own desires, I am not worthy of her affections. Now that I have broken her gaze, I learn to breathe again.

"You should go," I murmur. I do not know what else to say, but I know that if I allow her to stay too much longer, I will kiss her.

And that will not be a good thing.

"You want me to go?" Fiora asks, her question laced with meaning. I dig my nails into my palm. There are multiple answers to that question. *No. Never leave me. If you leave, I will feel even worse.* But I push those answers aside.

"Yes. It is late. It has been a long night," I force myself to say. In the corner of my eye, I see disappointment cross Fiora's face. I watch as she suppresses a sigh, gathering her supplies.

"Goodnight, then."

I do not respond to her as she leaves the room. The words catch in my throat. There is a sense of relief when she is gone, that I will not have to face up to how she makes me feel. Perhaps it will be enough to make her keep her distance. That will be for the best. She is better off without me dragging her down.

But the moment she goes, it feels like I might miss her forever.

Chapter Nine

I suppose I have been avoiding Fiora. After the moment between us the other night, I can barely face myself, let alone her. I have long since had a hard time staring at my reflection, but when I look at myself in the mirror this morning, I see what the rest of the world must. A woman unable to let anyone through the armor. A woman with her expression twisted by bitterness. A woman refusing to heal, even given the opportunity to change.

I can never seem to get it right. Fiora was trying her best to get closer to me and all I did was push her further away. She has been so patient with me, and yet now I can see that even her patience has its limits. I would opt not to speak to me too if I was her. It surprises me that she has stayed here at all. But though she hasn't visited the library in days, her friends still walk the halls, and there is still light coming from beneath her bedroom door. She may have given up on trying to know me, but she hasn't forgotten the promises she made me.

I should apologize. I stand now in the raven tower, staring out at my kingdom, thinking about how meaningless it all is. I have ruled this land for three years and not one of the people I have cared for has given me the time of day.

But a traveling witch with no loyalty to me has offered me a fresh start. Fiora did not judge me for my sins, for my anger, for my cruelty. She tried to understand me, and I have spent every moment since then proving everyone else's opinions of me to be right. I am monstrous. I am harsh and unlovable.

Maybe that is why I find it so hard to let her in. Because I know that I am bad at my core, like a rotten apple. Maybe because I know that she cannot possibly love me as I am, and the witch promised that I would only ever be free if someone loved me. It terrifies me that someone like her might be willing to give me a chance, and yet it still will not be enough. What if her lips ventured to meet mine, and nothing happened? What if the kiss only showed her how cold I am, starved of the warmth of love?

I cannot bear to imagine that moment. It would destroy me entirely. It is safer to keep my distance, to let her think there is some other way to help me. Maybe she will discover some other solution and I will not have to worry anymore that love is the only thing capable of saving me.

I hear a squawk as a raven approaches the window perch. I frown. I do not often receive ravens, and now they have come several times in one week. My stomach twists at the thought of another attack. I am weary from the last battle, and I need time to recover. But the raven holds out a letter in its beak and I know I must take it and face whatever it says.

But this does not appear to be a letter from the townsfolk. In fact, it seems like it could be from somewhere far away. There is a red emblem sealing it closed that I do not recognize right away. I open up the letter to see what it might say.

Queen Alana of Thornwood,

Please expect a visit from the representatives of Deepmoat within days of receiving this letter. King Griffin comes to you with a proposition that will join your kingdoms and create peace in the lands.

I read the letter several times, trying to figure out what this all means. What is this talk of peace? Thornwood has not been at war for many years, at least not with humankind. There is a reason that we have never had a real army, devoting our efforts instead to tending the lands of our goddess.

And what does the King of Deepmoat want with me? Surely this is not a marriage proposition? I have made it very clear to my subjects and to other kingdoms that I am not interested in marrying a man. Perhaps he is proposing a marriage of convenience, a marriage to bond our kingdoms, but why? What would we stand to gain?

I hear a horn outside and look out onto the road leading up to the castle. It seems my guests have arrived earlier than expected. I watch as a golden carriage trundles up the cobbled road, the horses inelegant as they pull my guest up the hill. I sigh. I suppose I will have to deal with this now and find out what this king wants.

But if he thinks he is leaving here with a wife, he has another thing coming.

I receive King Griffin in the throne room. I have not stepped in here once since my parents died. I never had a crowning ceremony, and I was never officially made into a queen. It felt wrong to sit where they once sat, especially since no one wanted me on the throne in the first place. Being a queen has been set aside in favor of simply getting out of the way.

But this special guest has called for me to take up my duties once again. I sit in the uncomfortable chair, my mother's golden crown of thorns sitting atop my head. The fact that it matches my thorned armor only makes me feel more uncomfortable.

King Griffin does not seem uncomfortable in the slightest. As he brings his entourage into the hall, he stands tall and arrogant. His blonde hair curls over his forehead, his armor shining like it has just been polished. He does not appear like someone who has been on the road for days. I suppose he must be trying to make a good impression. But the moment he scowls at me, looking me up and down, I know that he and I will not get along as friends.

"It is customary to rise for a king," he says through gritted teeth. I raise my eyebrows.

"You are in my kingdom now. I am the queen here. I do not believe I need to rise at all," I say. "And may I add that you have arrived with little notice at all. I do not believe you are following any etiquette rules when it comes to being polite."

He sneers at me. "So the rumors are true. You are as stubborn and cold as they say. But no matter. I will have plenty of time to change that."

Every word that comes out of his mouth is

both foul and equally surprising. If he came here to change me somehow, I think he is going to be very displeased with his results. I grip the edges of the throne and stare him down, glad that my chair is raised above him. At least I don't have to allow him to think we are equal here.

"State the purpose of your visit. I would very much like to get to the point," I tell him. I watch as he tries to arrange his face into something more pleasant, something less hostile. It does not work very well.

"I have something you need," he declares. I raise my eyebrow once more.

"Is that so?"

"I have one of the largest armies in all of the lands. I have men who have trained in combat since they were barely out of the womb."

"No women?" I butt in. I should not be surprised. Now that he has arrived, I am recalling who this man is. He is the man who single handedly caused his goddess - Koa, the goddess of war - to destroy his lands in a fit of rage. Now, he lives in godless lands with his army of child soldiers. *Male* soldiers only.

"Women do not fight as well as men. It is a fact," he insists.

"Do you realize you are speaking to the woman who single-handedly destroyed the plague of arachnids that scourged the lands? I do not believe anyone else can say the same."

"Perhaps you should allow me to finish what I am saying," King Griffin snarls. I sit back in my seat.

"Alright. But do hurry. I am tired of listening to one man be so wrong about so many things."

His face screws up in anger. "You need my army. I know you are having trouble with dark magic once again. You cannot seem to turn it away from your home. And I have an army that rivals in size to that of your enemies."

I resist the urge to sigh. "Since you seem to know so much about my situation, you will know that only magic can contend with the creatures darkening my doorstep. Your army of boy children will not do. So in fact, I do not believe you can help me after all."

"Quiet! Infuriating woman!" the king snaps. "You refuse to see my value to you, but you will regret that if you do not listen to me. Bad things are coming. Our kingdoms need to stand together."

I lean forward in my chair, examining him more closely. His reddened face is hiding something behind his eyes - fear. He is concerned for his own safety. Is it possible I am not the only one having issues with these monsters?

"If you believe your army is capable of handling the threat, then why are you here? I have no armies to speak of. What worth do you think I - *an infuriating woman* - have to you? You would not be here begging for my attention if you did not see some value in me."

King Griffin wavers. I sigh.

"I suppose you are basing your proposal here off these rumors you seem so familiar with. You believe that I am invincible, given what happened three years ago. You would like to send me onto the battlefield to fight for you, despite your belief that women have no place on the front lines, or anywhere if you had your way. So you want to marry me to use as your pawn. And you are arrogant enough to believe that your offer of marriage is a good trade off. An eligible bachelor such as yourself...I would be *mad* to refuse, is that what you believe?"

"If we were to marry-"

"I have no interest in marrying you, sir. Even if you had something to offer me, which you do not, I will never share my bed with a man. If I marry, it will be to a woman. If I marry, it will be for love. Not for some desperate trade off with a man who has lost the love of even his goddess. You insult me by even suggesting it."

The king is trembling with rage now. Perhaps I have gone too far, but I will not sit here and be insulted by this man who expects me to marry him and be grateful for it. I may not have the love of my own people, but I have done a good job of keeping them safe without the need of an arrogant man who cannot stand to believe women have purpose outside of the kitchen or the bedroom. He seeks to usurp me from my seat and have me say thank you after? Not a chance.

"You have no idea what you are doing," he hisses at me. "You humiliate me in front of your court-"

"Look around you. There is only me, you and your people here. I did not set out to humiliate you, but you came here with every intention of trying to undermine me and play me for a fool. You say that I need you, but it is clearly the other way around. If you wish to protect your people, then you need only ask for my help. I will offer what little I have. But I will not be your wife."

"You think you can do better than me?" he sneers, looking me up and down. I feel a familiar chill running through my body. That look he is giving me says everything I need to know. That by looking at me, he deems me inferior. He looks at my bigger stature, my untamed red hair, the scar down my face, and he believes I am ugly. He sees that I am trapped in this armor and he believes that on some level, I deserve it. I set my jaw, but he keeps prodding.

"You think that you are above me? I would be stooping to the lowest of the low to be with you. Monstrous woman…it sickens me to look at you. I must have been out of my mind to think I could marry a beast like you-"

The doors to the throne room fly open as though powered by a gust of wind. And then I see why.

Fiora is standing in the doorway, her eyes glowing golden as she strides toward Griffin. It takes me a moment to see that she is furious. Her usual soft smiles have been replaced by blazing eyes and flared nostrils. A wave of cold so strong that it almost penetrates through my armor flies in my direction. The king stumbles back a few steps, taken by surprise by the sheer force of Fiora's entrance.

"What did you just say to the queen?" she snarls. She holds up her hand and a naked flame appears on it. She thrusts it just beneath the king's chin so that the flames lick at his thin beard. He trembles where he stands, horrified.

"N-nothing…"

"You called her a beast! How dare you speak to her that way? How dare you speak to her at *all?* Who do you think you are?"

"Fiora…" I begin.

"Quiet! This will not stand!" she says, turning to me. Those golden eyes of hers have me shrinking back into my seat. She returns her attention back to King Griffin.

"You will apologize to the queen, and you will beg for mercy at her hand for what you have done. Let us hear it before I really set your pathetic beard alight!"

"I am sorry! I am sorry!" he cries out. Fiora closes her fist with flourish, extinguishing the flame.

"That is what I thought. Now leave. Do not darken Thornwood's doorstep again."

The king swallows, shaken as he looks at me in horror. But I cannot take credit for this display. I dismiss him with a wave of my hand.

"You need not return. Unless you really do want a war on your hands," I say. He sniffs, glaring me down.

"You will regret sending me away when the creatures come to call," he says, a tremble of fear and rage in his voice. I manage a small smile despite myself.

"I do not imagine that I will. As you can see, my kingdom is quite well protected."

Griffin shoots one last glance at Fiora, who still shakes with rage. Then he turns on his heel and leaves, his men falling in line behind him. I close my eyes as soon as the doors shut behind him. The presence of such an awful man has really taken it out of me.

I feel gentle hands on my own. When I open my eyes, Fiora is kneeling before the throne, her hand slipped into mine. Her rage has faded to a glimmer in her eyes. Now, she seems only concerned.

"Are you alright?" she asks me.

"Of course. He did me no harm."

Her forehead creases. "Words are just as sharp as swords."

I swallow. She sees right through me. She knows me better than anyone has in a long time. I turn my head away from her.

"It hardly matters. He was as much a monster as I am. But I wonder if he is right. He has a force larger than most. If I truly want to protect my people, perhaps I should have accepted his offer. I should not have been so rash."

"The only thing stronger than you is magic. That is the only thing that we can use to destroy these creatures," Fiora reminds me. "His army is of no use to us here. But I have been thinking…and I know this is not my place…but I do believe we need to seek out someone who knows dark magic better than us. If you will accept my help…I can take you to a witch who knows more on the subject than I do. If this is the work of darker forces…then perhaps she can help you defeat it." She pauses. "I know how your people feel about magic…but once again, it might be the only thing capable of saving them."

"I believe you may be right," I say with a sigh. "But I cannot leave my kingdom…I have not left in many years. I have to stay to rule."

"Alana…we both know you have been unable to rule properly for years. The people will handle themselves while we are gone. It will be close to a week's journey to reach the witch. She resides in Shadowwater and I know it is a long way…but I think it is necessary."

I ponder for a minute. Fiora's words ring true, and though I dislike the idea of leaving my kingdom unguarded, particularly after what just happened, it might be the only way.

"If it is the only way…then we shall leave in the morning," I say. Fiora nods, standing up and brushing herself off. She turns as though to leave, but it feels wrong for her to leave like this. After what she did for me, even after everything…

"Fiora?"

She turns back to me. Something in her expression looks hopeful.

"Yes?"

I swallow. "I want to thank you. For how you stood up for me. You are right…words have a sharpness of their own. You did not have to do that for me, though."

"I wanted to," she whispers. Her words hang in the air for a moment. My throat tightens.

"Thank you. I mean it."

She smiles softly. "Anything for you, dearest."

Chapter Ten

We prepare to leave in the morning before the sun has risen in the sky. Bolt is itching to leave, allowing me to attach the saddle to her back without any fuss. Now that she is fully grown, she is large enough to carry both Fiora and I on her back, plus our supplies. At first, I worried she would not take to it, given that we rarely leave the confines of the kingdom's walls, but I know that she is desperate to run, to see the world. Fortunately for her, we have places to be.

"I confess, I have never ridden on the back of a wolf before. Does she not mind it?" Fiora asks, stroking Bolt's fur. Many people get nervous around a wolf that is almost as big as them, but Fiora does not appear to be flustered. I think it takes a lot to shake her.

"She loves it," I say. "Just wait until the ride begins. She will be running faster than you can even imagine."

"Well, go steady, Bolt. It is a long journey. We

do not want you to tire your paws out," Fiora says, smiling down at my wolf. Bolt licks at her arm and she chuckles, making me smile. It is easy to forget that Fiora and I were barely speaking a few days ago. Now, everything seems back to normal. As normal as things can be with her around, anyway.

"Allow me to help you on the saddle," I tell Fiora. Before she can protest, my hands find her waist and lift her onto the saddle. The skirt of her cotton dress falls prettily either side of Bolt, making the whole thing seem much more elegant. It only reminds me that I am the opposite as I clamber onto the saddle in front of her. My stomach twists at the thought of us being so close for so long. With her face staring at the back of my spiked armor for hours on end, how can she possibly forget that I am cursed? That she should keep her distance?

"You will have to hold on to me. It is going to be a bumpy ride," I tell her. "But be careful of the armor-"

Before I can even finish speaking, her slender arms wrap around my waist, just below the point where the cursed armor ends. I can feel the ghost of her touch at the base of the breastplate. My face heats up until I am sure I am red hot to touch. I am glad she cannot see my face.

"Alright. I suppose we should go," I say, trying to compose myself. "Bolt...let us ride."

Bolt doesn't need to be told twice. One minute we are at a standstill. The next, Bolt is doing what she does best - bolting. Fiora lets out a surprised cry as we barrel toward the castle gates, propped open by Neville and Sigrid to allow us through. Their shocked faces pass by in a blur and I laugh as Bolt hurtles down the hill, Fiora clinging to me for dear life. At first, I worry that she is scared, that she is having second thoughts, but then I hear her joyous laugh in my ear and I grin. She is loving this as much as I am.

It feels good to ride Bolt again, and not into battle. I have rode her many times around the castle grounds, but nothing compares to this feeling, knowing she can run freer than she ever could before. We make it down the hill and pass through the town, where the townsfolk are just starting out their days. I am glad that for once, I do not have to endure the sight of their disgust at me, that I can leave them behind before they can inflict hurt upon me. And then, before I can process what is going on, I am out of the city limits and going beyond.

Bolt slows only a little, settling into a gallop. I hear Fiora collecting her breath behind me, realizing she is gripping me a little tighter than she was before. I cannot help but smile to myself. Fiora may be way too good for me, but it is nice to indulge in this beautiful woman holding me, just for once.

It falls upon Fiora to direct us. She gently tells Bolt where to go, guiding us through places just beyond my own borders, but places I have not seen since I was a child. When my parents were still alive, we would visit neighboring kingdoms, meet with the villagers, make trade deals with the kingdoms close by. I used to love it. It felt like I was seeing the world, before I knew just how big the world truly is.

But these places are unfamiliar to me now. When they heard of the Cursed Queen on their doorstep, they stopped extending their invitations to our kingdom. I try not to feel bitter as we pass them by, happier memories disappearing in a blur behind us as Bolt carries us through. Perhaps someday, I can mend what was broken. Perhaps once my curse is broken, I can make things right.

But why should I? I am always the one scrambling around attempting to pick up the shattered shards of the world around me. I tried my hardest to save my people, to save the kingdom, and I was met with hatred for it. So why do I still clamor for their favor? Why would I want to fix everything that is broken? My hands clutch Bolt's fur for comfort. I should be focussing on what I will say to the witch when we reach her. But the hurt inside me will not simply fade away. I have lived with it at my core for so long now that it feels permanent.

But it eases just a little as Fiora shifts her body closer to mine. Her thighs clamp around my legs from behind, her hands rested low beneath my breastplate. It makes me breathe a little easier. Right now, not much else matters to me.

We ride for a few long hours before Bolt begins to slow, panting for breath. It is easier to take in our surroundings now. Bolt is trotting along the dirt road atop a craggy mountain. Crisp salt air brushes my cheeks and I see that we are by the coast. Beyond the cliffs, stretching further than my eyes can see, are crashing waves and blue waters. My stomach twists. This is further than I have ever been from home before. I do not know where we are, but I know I want to see it.

"Stop, Bolt. Take a rest," I tell her gently. She slows to a halt, panting for breath. I struggle to get down from her back with grace, my legs wobbly from the long ride, but I am keen to explore. I offer my hand out to Fiora and help her to dismount, electricity crackling on my skin as our hands touch. She only seems to add to the magic of this place unknown to me. Bolt flops onto her side, completely worn out

"Where are we?" I ask Fiora. She looks around her with a smile.

"We should be in Shellshore. The kingdom is well known for its shellfish and seafood. Have you never been here before?"

"I have never been anywhere so far from home," I breathe, taking a few tentative steps toward the edge of the cliff. "This is my first time seeing the ocean."

It is magnificent. I have only ever read about it in books, and no words do justice to the wildness of it. It feels alive to me, each wave like a breath of life. The water is unlike anything from back home, glistening in the sun, unobscured by trees and low fog. Thornwood is beautiful in its own way, but this is different. I think of all of the life the waters hold, of the boats traveling across thousands of miles to other lands, to adventure. It unlocks a deep longing inside me for a life I have never seen, never lived. I always knew it was out here. But now that I see something so beautiful in front of me, not so far out of my reach, I realize just how much I have been missing out on.

"It is beautiful, is it not?" Fiora says, stepping up to join me at the edge of the cliffs. For reasons I cannot explain, my throat feels tight and tears spring to my eyes. I cannot remember the last time I cried, or was stirred to emotion this way, but something about the ocean, about this world I have been missing, has me choked up.

"It is," I manage to say. "It is beyond words."

"I have been here a few times before, to this kingdom. The first time was when I arrived here from Celestia," Fiora tells me. "I crossed the sea on a little boat with some of my sisters. It was terrifying at first. Trusting the waters to bring us here. But it was beautiful too. And when we arrived here, I tried shellfish for the first time. I took my first sips of wine. I kissed a woman for the first time. I am glad you got to see it here. It holds many good memories for me."

"I am glad to be here," I whisper. I cannot stop looking out at the waters. Where could they carry me if I let them? There is a whole world beyond here, and it feels as though it is opening itself up to me right now, showing me everything I have ever missed.

And then I feel Fiora's hand slip into mine. I forget to breathe for a moment. Even with my numbed sensations, I can feel how soft her hand is, how cool her palm is in mine like the kiss of seawater on my skin. I look at her and see how the gold on her skin shimmers now, even more beautiful than the ocean before me.

Her eyes are closed, breathing in the air, so I take the opportunity to simply watch her. There is something about her, something that stirs the humanity buried deep inside me. Something that gives me the ability to feel so much more when she is near. Would the ocean be quite so beautiful if she wasn't here to observe it with me? Would I even be able to appreciate the world around me without her beside me? It is like she brings it all to life, adds color where I can only usually see gray. It has to be the magic in her.

But maybe it is something more too. Perhaps I am coming to realize just how much she means to me in such a short space of time. How much she has changed me, changed the world around me. I see it now.

The world begins and ends with her.

"Tell me another. Please, Fiora, tell me another."

Fiora laughs. "I feel I am boasting."

"No, I want to hear it. That means it is not boasting. Please, Fiora. Tell me more."

We have set up camp for the night. I gathered some firewood and Fiora set it alight with little sparks from her delicate fingers. Now, we sit beside it sharing stories as Fiora eats. Mostly, though, I am intent on listening to Fiora's tales of her travels. I have no interest in talking about my past or my present. Both are far too sad. But stories of the world Fiora has seen? That I want to know about.

"Okay, I suppose I can tell you one more. But then we should rest," she says with a warm smile. I glance over to where Bolt is curled up beneath a tree, dead to the world and slightly snoring.

"Bolt will rest enough for the both of us," I insist. "Come on, Fiora. I am hungry for it."

She smiles. "Okay. Would you like to hear the tale of the day I left home? The day my eyes were filled with as much wonder as when you saw the ocean today?"

I nod. "Yes. I want to hear it."

"Well, then. As you know, I was raised in the Golden Palace of Celestia, along with my fellow young witches. We too never left the confines of the castle until we were ready. We had so much to learn before we could venture out and use our magic. But every young witch leaves Celestia when she is sixteen."

"Only sixteen? That seems so young…"

"You were only seventeen when you became queen, Alana."

"And I was far too young for the things I did, the things I saw. I was still a child…I had to grow up very fast."

Fiora's expression softens. "You had those things thrust upon you, I suppose. I knew all of my life that I would leave home at sixteen. And I felt well prepared for it. But nothing prepared me for the night I left the castle. There was one final stop where we all went together before we were sent out into the world. Just beyond our borders, there is a garden that is only visited by the recent graduates of Celestia's Golden Palace. Once a year, when the eldest girls leave, they are granted a night in this garden to explore their magic freely for the first time. The elder witches spoke of it often, calling it the Night of a Thousand Stars." Fiora's eyes close and a smile tugs at her lips.

"The garden was beyond beautiful. It was overgrown and wild, as nature should be. I walked barefoot through tall grass, through colorful wildflowers, through tiny fairies sitting atop moss covered rocks. I could feel the magic in the air around me like never before. And when the sky darkened, the fairies began to sing. The graduates danced and enjoyed the music, experimenting with the magic at our fingertips. But the night only truly began when the moon was high in the sky and midnight struck."

I lean forward, entranced by the story. Fiora opens her eyes and I can see the flecks of gold in her eyes shimmering in the light of the fire.

"The sky had never been clearer to me. Dotted with thousands upon thousands of stars, so bright they were almost blinding. The sky was white with them, as though it was the middle of the day. And for the first time, I was blessed with the presence of the goddess. I felt her all around me. Others around me continued to play with their magic, but I just lay down in the grass and felt how close she was to me. My skin tingled where it had been kissed by gold, her stardust. Her star may have exploded long ago, but it was then that I realized that she is alive and stronger than ever. She is all around us. She is dancing in the flames of every fire. She is whispering through the ocean. She is helping keep the rest of the stars shining." Fiora lets out a deep sigh, looking into my eyes. "I have seen the whole world that she bestowed upon us…but I have never been anywhere quite so enchanting as that garden. And the one curse of being shown it is that I am never allowed to return."

"Why not?"

"It is intended to be a once in a lifetime experience, carved out for our kind. I believe the point is to show us that beauty is where we look for it. That is why I never stay in one place too long. That is why I chose to continue to travel. The world has so much to offer. I want to see as much of it as possible before I return to the goddess. In fact…staying in the castle with you is the longest I have stayed put since I was sixteen."

I feel my face turn hot. I know she does not mean anything by her comment. She is simply stating a fact. She has stayed at my side because she has to, not out of choice. But knowing I have carved such a big piece of her time away feels special to me.

She is watching me now with a look in her eye that I cannot decipher. What is it that she wants me to say? She looks like she is expecting something. But words are her forte, not mine. I do not know what I can say to that. I clear my throat.

"It sounds as though you have been on a truly beautiful journey," I say, testing the words out on my lips. She reaches out to touch my face and I find myself exhaling, surrendering to her.

"A beautiful journey depends on the company you keep," she murmurs. I blink, feeling the urge to cry for the second time today. Is she telling me that she craves my company the way I crave her's? Or is she referring to her friends from the road? I cannot be certain. It feels too delicate to ask. How can I risk making things uncomfortable between us?

We have a long journey ahead of us. If keeping things neutral between us is what it takes to retain peace and harmony, then that is how it must be. I clear my throat, turning my gaze away from her.

"You should rest," I say gently. "I will keep watch of our camp. You will be safe."

Fiora hesitates, her thumb brushing my cheek. Some part of me wishes that she would turn my face back to her. That she would lock me in a kiss that I have no desire to escape from.

But she doesn't. She sighs quietly.

"I do not doubt it," Fiora says, her face unreadable. She drops her hand away from my face, her eyes lowering, shrouded by her long, dark lashes. "Goodnight, Alana."

I swallow. "Goodnight."

I hastily help her set up a pillow to sleep upon made from our supply bag and she curls up beside the fire, her back turning on me. I let my shoulders sag. It is better this way. Safer. I lean my back against a nearby tree, my night watch beginning. The least I can do is keep Fiora safe through the night. And as she sleeps, I have plenty of time to remind myself that I am nowhere near good enough for her.

I would do well to remember my place.

Chapter Eleven

It takes another four days of intense travel for us to reach the witch's home in Shadowwater. The morning after we told our tales around the campfire, Fiora was pleasant, but she had put a certain distance between us once again. Perhaps she had expected something more from me. I guess I will never know.

But I do know that I still think about her. When we are riding Bolt silently through kingdoms unknown to me and lands I long to explore, I think of her and the life she leads on the road. I crave it. I crave *her* along with her life.

And yet I know it can never be while I still bear this curse, or while I still have a kingdom to rule, a sense of duty binding me. She has always had free reign of her life and her choices, but the same cannot be said for me. Until something changes, she must remain a fantasy that I refuse to indulge in.

And where love is concerned, I know that only a true love can break my curse. I know that Fiora has had lovers in lands all across the world. She may care for me, she may not. But if she is not my true love, which seems doubtful, then things could never work between us anyway. That is enough to make me keep her at arm's length. That way neither of us get hurt.

She is also a distraction from the real issues at hand. If the creatures that plague my kingdom cannot be stopped then my people will be doomed. Like it or not, they need me. And as soon as I reach the witch who might have answers for me, I can at least try and save them one more time. That is my burden to bear, not Fiora's. Unlike me, she can walk away from this at any time. Given how tense things have been these past few days, I am beginning to think she will go sooner rather than later.

The witch we seek lives by the sea. We have been hugging the coast for days now, the sea salt crusting in my hair and making it more unruly than ever. As we grow closer to our destination, a deep fog rolls in too, not unlike the ones back at home. I can see why this place is known as Shadowwater. But finally, I see where she resides as the mist clears, giving me an opening to what lies ahead.

There is a small island out in the open waters,

a gray stone house standing upon it proudly. It looks a little bleak out there alone, storm clouds gathering over it as though sensing the purpose of our visit. But I am determined to get there quickly and figure out how to end our troubles back home.

"How do we get to it without a boat?" I ask Fiora, squinting to look at the island. "Swimming there seems like a bad idea…"

"We will just have to be patient. When the tide goes out, a path will appear," Fiora says. I shift from foot to foot, keen to make that happen sooner than I think is likely.

"When will that be?"

"I am not sure…I have only visited once, long ago. The path was clear then."

I am about to ask more questions when I hear the waves crashing louder than before. I turn my sights to the ocean and, to my horror, I see that the waters are being manipulated by some force beyond nature, shoving water aside until a wall of water that could almost touch the clouds appears. I stare down the now exposed pathway to the house and see that a woman is standing outside it now, her hands raised in the air. I look at Fiora in disbelief.

"Is she doing that?"

Fiora smiles. "I believe so."

"Could *you* do that?"

"Perhaps in my wildest dreams," she laughs, leading the way to the sodden pathway. The waves have formed an aquatic tunnel for us to walk through, and I cannot put aside my nerves as we pass by. Fiora openly admires the witch's handiwork as we pass through.

"Petra has powers far beyond my own. If I attempted something so bold, it would exhaust me. But she does not look tired to me."

Nor to me either. As we walk closer, I can see that Petra is older than the other witches I have met. I know that many witches live for hundreds of years if they are powerful enough, and given what Petra seems capable of, she must be very old indeed. She has silvery white hair that flows below her waist and sways in the wind. Her face is creased with age, cheeks flushed by years of sun, but her body stands strong even after such a long life. She is stunning in so many ways that I cannot help staring at her.

"You must know it is rude to stare, Alana of Thornwood," she says as we approach. I blink.

"How…how do you know who I am?"

"Child, I can part the sea with just my hands. I can do things beyond your most fanciful imaginings," she says. Bolt howls as Petra finally allows the water to cascade back into place, leaving us trapped upon the island. I soothe

Bolt with a gentle stroke of her head, but I do not feel particularly at ease myself.

"I am not sure if you remember me…" Fiora says, looking a little shy as she faces Petra.

"Of course I remember you. It feels like only minutes since I saw you last," Petra says, cupping Fiora's cheeks. "I remember all the young witches who pass by my home. You seemed especially promising."

"That is so kind of you to say…though I fear I will never live up to your standards," Fiora says with a blush.

"Do not be so sure. You are so young. You have many years ahead of you to explore your magic. But I sense that right now, time is not on your side. Come inside, both of you. And bring your lovely wolf with you, Alana. Tell her only to wipe her paws on the way in."

Bolt pants, brightening up once again. We approach the house and enter, me holding my breath. The last time I visited a witch's home, she put a curse on me that ruined my life. I only hope that the visit to see Petra will be less damning.

Inside her home is certainly more welcoming. It looks almost ordinary, save for the collection of herbs and spices on a rack above a bubbling cauldron in the kitchen. A small black cat slinks by and approaches Bolt, sniffing her curiously. I hold my breath, hoping Bolt will not do anything that might get us kicked out, but the cat simply walks away in disinterest while Bolt's ears sag. Petra turns to see the interaction and kneels in front of Bolt to pet her.

"Such a lonely creature," she murmurs. "Just like her owner."

I blush. I hate the way she is reading me. She knows too much. Next she will be telling Fiora that I am falling for her. Petra stands and winks at me before offering us a seat at her table. I take one, avoiding her eyes. It is starting to feel as though she can read my mind, so perhaps I had better tread lightly from here on forward.

"Please do not worry yourself, Alana," Petra says to me. "You are safe here. No harm will befall you."

"I was told that you know dark magic better than anyone. If that puts me a little on edge, I do apologize," I say gruffly. Fiora shoots me a look but Petra does not seem to be fazed.

"Yes, I know dark magic. But I do not practice it. Not for many many years," she said. "You see, magic is not black or white, Alana. Any witch is capable of dark magic. It is not stronger than good magic. It is only more deadly, more cruel. Witches do not simply have it or not. They choose the path to dark magic, and it changes them. Not the other way around."

"Petra turned her back on dark magic long before we ever existed," Fiora says firmly. "She lives her exile out here, only taking visitors from young witches who need her help. Do not assume to know who Petra is just because she knows of dark magic."

I bow my head. "My apologies. Magic is not something that I know much about."

"That is quite alright. You were taught to be wary of it. Your parents made you believe it is evil. And it can be. But as I said. Nothing is black and white. Now, perhaps you can tell me why you are here? Though I can guess already what you are looking to find out."

"Three years ago, I defeated an army of creatures intent on destroying my kingdom and everything around it," I tell her. "I asked an exiled witch known as Laurel to help me, and she did. She enabled me to kill the army and bring peace to my lands. But now they are back and they are…well, they are more difficult to kill."

"They seemed immune to blades," Fiora adds. "Only magic could send them to their graves. It led me to believe that dark magic must be involved."

"Yes. Dark magic is the only thing capable of preventing death and making skin impenetrable.

To manipulate what lives or dies can never lead to anything good.," Petra agrees. She glances at me. "You should know, Alana. I see your past loud and clear in my mind. You took a curse to fight them, did you not?"

"I had to save my people."

"Oh, I do not judge you. The lure of dark magic's potential enchants the best of us. It certainly enchanted me long ago. You have not indulged in magic since?"

"No."

"And you still bear your curse? Your armor?"

"Not just that. I…I do not feel much. Emotionally or physically."

"I see. Laurel stripped you of the things that you believe add up to your humanity. A cruel trick for someone attempting to do good," Petra says sympathetically. "Do you believe she may be behind these new attacks?"

"I believe it is possible. Laurel despises the people of Thornwood for exiling her into the woods. She has grown bitter in her years alone. She wanted me to free her once I became queen…but I never did."

"Ah. Well, I can see how she might feel slighted in that case. It sounds highly likely that she is the one behind the attacks. She will be fully aware that the only thing that can stop these creatures is magic. She means to destroy your kingdom."

"What can I do?" I ask desperately. "If I cannot protect my people, then what am I good for? And though Fiora is strong, she cannot fight alone. There has to be some way for me to stop the witch's powers."

"You are right. There is a way to stop her. You can stop her powers at the source," Petra says darkly. Fiora's eyes widen.

"You surely do not suggest that we kill this witch? She is thousands of years old and more powerful than all of us combined…"

"I do not appreciate the implication that her powers stretch beyond mine, Fiora. But you are likely right. She may not be more powerful…but it seems that she is willing to do whatever she can to bring herself power. That makes her more dangerous. She has nothing to lose. Which is why it is even more important that you should kill her. For as long as she remains alive, no one can truly be safe."

"And how do you propose we kill a witch of such power?" I ask, raising an eyebrow. "You said that only magic can compete with magic. I do not have those abilities."

"Perhaps not, Alana. But you are a very gifted fighter. You need not wield magic yourself. You only need a weapon blessed by magic. Show me your sword."

I unsheathe my longsword and place it on the table for Petra to examine. She hums to herself and nods.

"A fine sword. And absorbent," she declares. I frown.

"Absorbent?"

"Of magic," Fiora says quietly. "But Petra...do you think this is the only path? I do not want blood to spill."

Petra's face softens. "Sweet child...blood will always spill. You must choose whose it shall be...the innocent people of Thornwood and beyond, or the witch intent on torturing people. If she dies, her magic dies." Petra turns to me. "You have been looking for ways to break your curse, have you not? Ending Laurel's life will free you too."

My eyes widen. "It will?"

"Of course. The power she currently holds over you will cease to exist. She told you there was only one way out...but this is the other. I can guess why she did not tell you about this."

I mull over how much I want this. Killing Laurel may have benefits, but it also has plenty of problems. First off, I would have to defeat a powerful witch with no idea what I might face. Second of all, killing her would remain on my conscience forever. I have never sought to hurt another person before. We may be different, and Laurel may have ruined my life, but does that mean I am willing to end her life?

"The choice is yours, Alana," Petra tells me firmly. "Allow me to bless your sword. You do not have to use it if you so wish."

"Could we not simply kill the creatures with the sword?" Fiora asks desperately. "To hurt another witch…it feels unthinkable."

"You could. But both of you may die in battle. There will be no magic that can protect Alana so fully this time…I am not willing to shield her the way Laurel did. If the creatures come in force, you will both be in danger. I know you wish to remain on the purest path, Fiora. But even walking on a path of goodness can be muddy at times."

"I understand," I tell her. "Please…if you are willing to bless my sword…then do it. I will face the witch myself. I will offer her a way out. And if she does not take it…then I will do what is needed of me."

"Very good," Petra says. One of her bony hands reaches to touch the sword. "This could take some time. Please, feel free to explore the island. I will be done by sunrise in the morning."

"Thank you. I appreciate your help," I say graciously. Bolt, who has been waiting by the door, sits up eagerly as I approach and step back out onto the island. I nod to her.

"Go on. Run and play."

Bolt runs off in a flash, chasing a flock of birds that have settled on the grass of the island. I sigh, feeling the burden of what I must do weighing down on my shoulders. I sit alone for a while, and I wonder if Fiora is trying to dissuade Petra from this dark plan. I do not like it either. I have no desire to kill Laurel.

But if it is the only path, then I will take it.

After some time, Fiora leaves the house and comes to sit beside me. I know by the look on her face that she will have something to say about the matter.

"What would you have me do? Do you see a way out?" I ask her. She wavers, staring out at the ocean. The waves are still rough, crashing against the shore as a storm grows ever closer.

"I cannot say what I would do in your shoes," Fiora says. "I only know that I desire peace above all else."

"And I intend to bring it back to my home," I tell her firmly. I take a deep breath. "It is not your burden to bear. And now that I know how to end this once and for all...you are free of your duty to me too."

Fiora's head snaps to the side so she can meet my gaze. "What can you possibly mean?"

"Fiora...the only reason you are here in the

first place is because you promised not to leave until you helped me escape my curse. Now, we have found the solution. I can kill two birds with one stone when I face Laurel. You are free to leave now."

"The only reason? Is that what you believe? That I stayed because I felt I had to?" Fiora demands. She tries to glare into my eyes and I look away. "You know that is far from the truth. I see the way you twist and turn to avoid looking me in the eye, to avoid admitting what you really want…do not be a coward, Alana. Tell me what really irks you."

I force myself to look into her eyes. "I have no idea what other reason you would have to drag yourself down to my level. Does it tell you nothing that my own people hate me? That I have been alone for all these years?"

"That is no fault of your own. Your people are ignorant and old-fashioned. They refuse to see how you helped them because you used magic. That has nothing to do with your character. I care for you, Alana. Surely you can see that by now? If I had no feeling for you at all, would I keep fighting to be close to you, to help you? Do you truly believe I would have stayed simply because I *owed* you?"

"I am no good for you!" I cry out. "I am nothing. Nothing at all."

"Do not say such things. I will not hear it."

"I am nothing good. You choose not to believe it, but I know myself. I am a thorn among roses. I ruin everything. I hurt everyone I touch. I am no good, no matter how I try. I cannot be better until the curse is gone…"

"Have you ever considered that you cursed yourself the day you decided to believe the nonsense you are spewing?" Fiora snaps. "You have never been any of those things. You took what you see on the outside and made yourself believe you are the same inside. You see the thorns on your armor and turn them inwards to yourself. You are *good*. Why can you not look inside yourself for once and see who you truly are?"

My throat feels tight. I never expected this to escalate this way. I had no idea she would care enough to fight me like this. I open my mouth to speak, but for once, I have no voice. Could she be right about me? Have I done this to myself?

I clench my fists. No. Even if she is right, it does not matter. It changes nothing. I still have to face the witch. I will likely die trying. And even if I break the curse, even if I kill the witch, I will still have to face an army of monsters once again. This time, there will be no magic to protect me, and I will not risk Fiora dying on the battlefield to help me. It is becoming clear to me that however things pan out, there is no happy ending in store for us.

Unless we are parted.

It is time that she and I go our separate ways. If it has to be on bad terms to make her go, then so be it. If it keeps her safe from the war on my kingdom's doorstep, then I am willing to endure the hurt in my heart when she walks away.

I dig my nails into my palm. I know that I have to be cruel to be kind. Fiora is as stubborn as I am. She will not leave unless I give her a good reason to. I close my eyes for a moment, and when they reopen, I harden my expression.

"Whatever you think you know about me, you are wrong," I say darkly. "I told you, I am incapable of feeling anything at all. You mean nothing to me, and I suggest you walk away before you hurt your own feelings."

Fiora's forehead creases. "I know what you are attempting to do. It will not work on me."

"Leave before you force me to do something cruel."

"Something crueler than trying to break my heart?" Fiora asks. For the first time, I see the cracks beginning to show. There is a wobble in her voice. It makes my stomach twist. But I cannot give in to her. She may hate me for it, but I am saving her life. There is no sense in us both losing our lives for a war that does not belong to her. I keep my eyes hard.

"If I must, I will," I say. The words are like thorns in my throat, choking me. Fiora keeps looking at me for a while, but then she presses her lips into a thin line and breaks eye contact.

"So be it. We will do it your way," she murmurs. I watch her begin to walk toward the water and I panic. Surely she doesn't mean to swim?

But then I watch something that astonishes me. With a cry of rage, she lifts her hands in the air. Slowly, but surely, the water begins to part, just like it did before. I watch as she storms across the open pathway, her hands shaking a little, but holding the walls of water steady. She was so sure that she would be incapable of such a feat, but I suppose anger makes us do things beyond our own imaginings.

When she reaches the other side, I allow myself to fall to my knees, tears falling down my cheeks. Watching her go feels impossible, but I know it is the right thing to do. My heart breaks to imagine that I will never see her again. I grip the grass beneath me, wishing I could scream and let out all the hurt building inside me. After so long feeling numb, this broken heart of mine is too much to bear.

But I only need to survive this pain a few more days. Once I face the witch, my fate will be sealed. No pain will follow me any longer. I will finally be free of it.

Even if I do not live to appreciate it.

Chapter Twelve

I have a long while to sit with my thoughts on the lonely island, waiting for Petra to work on the sword. Now that Fiora is gone, I can think of little other than her. It should be a welcome distraction from what I must face when I return home, but knowing that I let the one good thing in my life walk away is no blessing. I hug my knees, staring out at the ocean waves while Bolt nuzzles my side, trying to comfort me. She must be able to sense the turmoil within me. But I did this to myself. I have no one else to blame.

The only small comfort is that this will not matter for much longer. The bigger picture pushes aside my whimsical thoughts of romance and love. I will die in a few days time and what I want will cease to matter. I may not make my peace with it, but I know that is the only outcome.

Daylight returns before Petra appears from inside her cabin, holding my sword delicately in two hands. She looks weary now, and I wonder what kind of magic she has been working with to drain her in such a way. I stand and she offers the sword out to me.

"This sword holds immense power now," she warns me. "The kind of power that can rival a witch like Laurel. If you can get close enough to kill her…then you may be able to end this trouble of yours."

"What about the creatures?"

"As soon as the witch is dead, they should return to their natural forms, assuming she is the one behind their invincibility. The same applies to your curse. You will be free."

I nod, but I am not concerned about the curse right now. I doubt I will make it far enough for it to matter.

"Thank you. For everything you have done. I hope it is enough to save my people," I tell Petra. She nods and glances over my shoulder pointedly.

"Fiora is gone?"

I sigh. "Yes."

"You pushed her away."

I frown. Petra is far too nosy. A smile forms over her face and I know that she has heard my thoughts. That is something I struggle to get used to.

"I understand why you did. But I also sense

that you have spent a long time beating yourself up, Alana. When was the last time you allowed yourself to treat yourself with kindness?"

I roll my eyes. "Why should I? No one else does. That pattern alone makes me think that perhaps I am undeserving of it."

"But there was one person who treated you with kindness, was there not? You may have forced her to go, to walk away, but she would have gone to the ends of the earth with you. I think you know that."

I swallow, my eyes casting downward. That is the last thing I need to hear right now. I slide the sword back into its sheath, ignoring the look that Petra is giving me.

"I should be on my way. My kingdom needs me."

Petra nods. "Alright. But you remember what I told you. Remember that once you have defeated this enemy that you need to stop making an enemy of yourself. I wish you well in your endeavors."

"Thank you. Truly," I say, bowing my head respectfully to her. Petra walks me to the edge of the water and summons up the last of her energy to part the ocean once again. I shudder as I walk, still thinking about how Fiora managed to do the same only hours ago. Did her power come from her anger, as mine so often does? Magic and emotion seem to entwine from my experience. I hate to think that her capabilities came from a place of anger. Anger at me.

Bolt follows me closely to the other side of the water. When I turn back, I watch the water crash back into place, and when it does, Petra has already disappeared back inside. I am weary from the day's events, but I know that it is time to start the long journey home. Some part of me prays that I might come across Fiora on my way, that I might be able to take her home with me. But as Bolt and I ride, I do not see another soul. We ride even faster now than when Fiora was here, but the ride certainly feels lonelier.

We rest for a few hours in the afternoon so that Bolt can nap, and then we continue on home. We ride through the day and into the night until Bolt needs to stop again. Those parts of the journey are the worst. While she sleeps, I am reminded once again that I am alone, sitting with only my thoughts for company. I guess I was getting used to having someone to talk to, someone to laugh with, someone to pass the time with.

Get a grip, I tell myself, *you told her you were a monster. At least commit to it and put your feelings aside.*

But my feelings stay with me the whole way

home. Days pass in near silence, with only Bolt to break it up. Each passing hour makes it harder to stay above water, to stop myself drowning in my own misery. I almost wish for the days where I felt nothing at all. But Fiora changed all of that. No curse could ever numb the way she made me feel. How she will always make me feel.

I guess love truly is the strongest magic after all.

When Thornwood finally comes back into view, I truly feel as though I am broken. At least the kingdom has survived my absence by the look of things.. But as I ride back through the streets of the village up to the castle, I notice that everyone is inside their homes. Some of them have boarded their windows, and there is an eerie silence resting over the place. I shudder. It looks as though everyone is preparing for the war.

But only I can win it for us.

The castle is not a welcome sight to me. It feels like returning to a prison cell. But this may be the final time I ever see it. If the witch kills me, I need never return here.

I return to my bedroom one final time to don the rest of my armor. It will do little to help me against the witch, but I hide behind it regardless.

When I head back downstairs, preparing to

journey into the forest and meet with the witch, I am surprised to find Calla and Sigrid waiting in the hall, both of them talking in hushed voices. They jump as they notice me, relief crossing their faces. Sigrid strides over to me and thrusts a piece of parchment into my hands.

"We have been waiting for you to return…things have taken a turn since you left," Sigrid says darkly. "This is a message from King Griffin. His kingdom was attacked several days ago by the creatures. We have not received another raven since."

My stomach twists. If his kingdom was attacked, then I have no doubt in my mind that his home has been wiped out. All those young soldiers will have fought bravely, but winning was impossible without the use of magic. No wonder the people of Thornwood have opted to hide.

It also means we are running out of time. If I do not handle this soon, then we will be next.

I know I must go now. I must make my final sacrifice so that everyone else will live. I swallow, my sights set on the doors.

"I will handle this," I say, striding away. I do not want to explain to them what I mean to do. But they do not seem keen to allow me to get away so easily.

"Where is Fiora?" Sigrid asks, grabbing the

exposed part of my wrist to avoid touching my armor. I swallow, bowing my head.

"She left ahead of me. She will likely be traveling on foot. I imagine she will arrive when this is all over."

"What are you talking about? What are you going to do?"

I take a deep breath. I have to be honest. I owe them that, at least. "I have to journey to the woods. The witch who cursed me...I believe she is behind all of this. Petra told us that if we kill her, then the creatures she is fuelling with magic will be vulnerable once again. Only then do we have a chance."

"Then allow us to help..."

"No," I say firmly. "Stay here, wait for Fiora's return. Ensure she is safe. And then keep an eye on the raven tower. If the villagers need help, you may offer it. But keep yourselves safe. There is no sense in all of us dying for nothing."

"You do not mean to sacrifice yourself?" Calla whispers. "Alana...there has to be some other way around this."

I swallow. Why does she care anyway? She barely knows me. She is here for Fiora, as are the others. I am not their concern. I harden my expression. "I will not go down without a fight. But the witch in question is more powerful than I can compete with. I do not see myself living to tell the tale." I pause, trying to swallow down the lump in my throat. "I will go now. It is time to finish this. When Fiora returns…tell her…"

I cannot seem to form the words. *Tell her that I love her. That I am sorry,* I want to say. But speaking those words aloud will only make this harder. I have to shed my pain, my wants, my dreams. I have to treat this as the last time I will be here. I cannot burden Fiora with my feelings after I am gone. It is too cruel.

"Tell her to stay safe," I say eventually. I pull away from Sigrid's grip and walk away.

Calla calls after me, but I toss aside the letter from King Griffin and carry on walking. Bolt tries to follow me and my stomach squeezes. I have not had time to consider what to do about her. I do not want to see her die at the hand of the witch. It occurs to me that I cannot have her come with me.

I pause and kneel down beside her, burying my hands in her fur. Her head cocks, seeming to sense that something is wrong. I look into her eyes, my throat tight. This is goodbye.

"You are staying here," I tell her. It gives me deja vu of three years ago, telling her to run from the battle. But this time she growls, baring her teeth. She is too damn loyal. She wants to be at my side. But I shake my head, tears clogging my throat.

"Not this time, my girl. You have to stay. I love you too much to bring you this time. Keep the castle safe. Keep Fiora and her friends safe. Do as you are told, please."

She whines again, nipping my fingers as though she is trying to shock some sense into me. But I will not be swayed. I stand up, trying not to look at her as I go. I can hear her cries long after I leave the castle grounds and head to the forest.

It hurts. More than I thought possible. To walk away from my own life when it was finally starting to seem okay again. Away from the people I love. But perhaps this is a good thing. Fiora has changed me. I can feel it in me. She has made me better, no matter how monstrous I still see myself as. She has reminded me of the person I was three years ago. The woman willing to sacrifice herself to save her people, no matter the cost. And now it is time to do it again. Without Fiora, I think I would simply turn my back on those people as they did with me. Now, as the trees bow over my head and block out the sun, I embrace the darkness. I embrace what I have to do.

I have to do what is right.

Chapter Thirteen

The witch's cabin is just as I left it. If I hadn't had to endure three long years of loneliness because of my curse, it might feel as though I never left. I should have known that all paths would lead me back here. I draw my sword, on the defensive already. I want to talk with Laurel, to try and stop what she is doing. But I have a feeling that she will refuse to back down.

And then I will have to end her life.

As I move toward the cabin, the door swings open, though there is no sign of Laurel. I swallow. She must know why I am here. She wants to play with me, to make me fearful. But I have lived in fear long enough. There is nothing she can do to me now that she has not already inflicted upon me.

I step inside the cabin and see the witch waiting for me. She looks even stranger than she did before, her hair wilder, her body engulfed with moss and dirt. She grins at me.

"Cursed Queen...I have waited so long for you to return. I have missed you."

"You forced my hand. I had to come."

She shrugs with a mischievous smile on her face.

"You could have walked away from it all. I know these years have not been easy on you."

"You saw to that."

"Come now. I told you there would be consequences to your actions. I gave you what you wanted." Her smile fades from her face. "But you never gave me what I deserved."

I grip my sword harder. "Perhaps I will today."

She cackles. "Oh, sweet child. Do you really think you can defeat me? Just you and your little sword? I have lived for thousands of years. You cannot simply end me."

"That is not what I want. I want to spare you. But first, you have to call off the attacks on our kingdom. On *every* kingdom. Thousands will die."

"Oh, I know. Why do you think I am doing this?" Laurel says, straightening up. "Alana…magic has been shunned into the darkness for too long. For all of our power, we are forced to hide it, to act as though we are the same as everyone else. I will not bear it any longer. I want my sisters to be able to come out of hiding, to resume their true way of life in the world. But for that to happen…the rest must be wiped away."

I take a step toward her, falling down on my knees. "Laurel…please…"

"You intend to beg and make false promises again, Alana? Forgive me if I no longer trust you and your intentions."

"All I ever wanted was to stop people dying. Nothing has changed. Please, Laurel. It does not have to be this way."

"Oh, but it does. You and your people turned your back on me long ago. You made a mockery of me. Unless I do something, nothing will change. I gave you a chance once to end it, and you threw it back in my face. I suppose these three years felt long to you, but I have not wasted a moment of this time. I have been preparing my move. All you had to do was come back, make good on your promises. But you never did. And now, you are faced with the consequences again." She kneels in front of me, leveling out our faces. Up close, I do not see madness in her eyes. I see reason. I see calm. She reaches out and tries to take my sword. "But I am willing to give you another chance. You are different, Alana. You were willing to use magic to save your people. You were willing to bear a magical curse to make it happen. And now, I sense that magic has changed you once again…you fell in love with a witch, did you not? I can smell it on you."

I say nothing, my head bowed to the ground. She tries again to take my sword, but I grip it hard.

"Imagine a world where your love has no reason to hide. Where the woman you love can come into her power without consequence. Perhaps she will break your curse for you. You can start over. And all of those people who shunned you, who left you alone in the dark…they will cease to exist."

I close my eyes. I hate what she is promising. She wants so many people to die just so that she can live how she wishes. But she is offering to solve all of my problems. Temptation is a cruel hand tugging at me, trying to pull me into the darkness.

"No…my sacrifices…they meant something. If all of those people die…then what was it all for?"

"A lesson in how unfair this world can be. They had their chances too. They refused to let balance restore, for us all to live in harmony. And now it is my turn to tip the balance. Do you see, child? This is no act of evil. It is just a turning of the tables. Do not give another thought to those who do not deserve it. Join me. We can make it right again."

It would be so easy. To give into Laurel's power, to let her take the reins. She makes an argument so good that I could perhaps live my days in peace, wipe my conscience clean of whatever she does to take what she wants. The people of Thornwood are cruel and bitter and vengeful. I would not miss them.

But I am not willing to condemn them all. Despite all they have done to hurt me, I will not be the reason they all die. I raise my eyes to meet Laurel's.

"It is not my place to decide the balance of the world," I say, pulling my sword from the witch's grip. She gasps as the blade slices through her palm. I watch as gold beads of blood rise to the surface. She looks shocked that the sword is capable of hurting her. She thought herself to be invincible. Now, she sees that I truly mean to kill her. Her eyes darken and she rises up from her knees to her full height, towering over me.

"Then I shall do it alone," she snarls. She lets out a wild scream, the kind of scream that makes it feel like the walls are going to collapse inward. I stumble back, horrified, but I prepare myself for a fight.

I will not surrender so easily.

Laurel raises her hands to the ceiling, her

fingers curling inward to her palms as though she is gripping the air. I watch in horror as the tattoos on her skin glow golden. I know now that she is about to unleash hell on me.

With a yell of fury, she pushes her hands forward, unleashing a gust of wind so forceful that I fall flat on my back, almost dropping my sword. She screeches and a thousand bugs seem to appear from the woodwork, scuttling toward me and making me rush to leap up on the table to escape them. She cackles and another bolt of energy seems to leave her body, a bright white light that narrowly misses me. It occurs to me that one wrong move will end my life.

But she seems keen to toy with me first, to show off what she can do. She dances around the room, unleashing random bouts of magic. A vine snakes from her hand and wraps around my ankle, dragging me from the table and pulling me through the sea of bugs that have invaded the floor. Horrified, I hack at the vine with my sword to release myself. Laurel has already moved on, maniacally setting the place alight with bolts of fire. The walls of her cabin go up in flames and the bugs begin to flee, but I am still trying to catch my breath as black smoke fills the room.

"You will never match me, Cursed Queen. You are nothing. You have always been nothing," she snarls, her laughter dying and transforming into something more cruel. She douses the fires with jets of water, but the smoke remains, making me cough. I get to my feet, sword ready, but the chaos around me is making it hard to know how to proceed.

"You will die here for your efforts," Laurel cries, summoning another jet of water and forcing it upon me. Cold water hits my face, choking me, drowning me. My ears are muffled, but I can just about hear her.

"You will die alone. Without love. I hope that is the last thing you think of before you die."

My throat constricts. I cannot see, I cannot hear, swallowed by the water, but I feel the sting of what she said. Fiora's face comes to my mind, a golden angel through the pain. For a while, I was not so alone. For a while, my existence meant something. She gave me that.

And I pushed her away.

I scream into the water, the sound of my voice garbled and swallowed whole. I cannot die here. I cannot allow her to win.

The sword remains in my hand. I only have to get one good shot. I manage to open my eyes, the pressure of the water falling away from me as Laurel moves on to her next trick. This is my one and only opening.

I run for her. She hisses, seeing that I am

finally trying to retaliate. Those vines escape her hands once again, trying to ensnare me, but I slash them as I run, dodging around them. I make as though to leap on her, but I change course at the last minute, diving once more for the table. I grab her by her long hair, pulling her body against my spiked armor. She gasps in shock as her back feels the spikes dig into her skin, my sword pressing to her throat. I stop, panting for air. I want to give her one final chance. I want her to know she still has a choice.

"Surrender. Make things right," I cry out. Laurel's chest heaves as she breathes hard.

"I would rather die!"

I close my eyes. I am left with no choice. I cry out as my sword slices through her skin. She does not make a sound. I feel her body fall away from me, out of my grip. But when I finally open my eyes, there is no sign of her. All that is left is a golden dust in the air, sparkling in the haze of the ruined cabin.

I let out a sob. I cannot believe it is over, that I killed a woman who has lived a thousand years. I gasp for air as I cry, holding out my hand to touch the remains of the woman born of the goddess of the sky. It should never have been this way.

And the worst part is, she was right about

many things. The unfairness of this world. The imbalance of it all.

"I wish it could have been different," I choke out. But she is gone. She cannot hear my words.

And as my tears fall, something begins to change. I gasp as I feel the breastplate of my armor detach itself from my skin. I look down and watch as the magical thorns that formed on the armor retract once again. I feel sensation coming back to my body. The remaining heat from the burning walls fires up my cheeks. I can feel my hand gripping the sword that ended Laurel's life. I can feel the sting of the salt tears in my eyes. I was told that only love could save me, that I would live with my curse until I found it.

And yet now I am free.

My lungs feel alive again. Smoke curls into them and I know I need to get out of the cabin before the smoke kills me. After everything that has happened, I cannot bear to lose everything now. I make for the door, leaving Laurel behind me. Fresh air makes me gasp a little. I can feel the breeze on my skin. I can smell autumn in the air.

I am alive. Truly alive.

Chapter Fourteen

My lungs are burning as I run back to the town. Now that Laurel is dead, the creatures can be killed, but that will surely not prevent them from trying their onslaught yet again.

But this is the third and final time I will face them. If I survive another day, it will only be once all of them are gone, once and for all.

It becomes clear to me as I near the neat rows of houses in Thornwood village that there is something amiss. I can hear screaming, and I see one of the large creatures clambering its way over the vine wall. I brace myself. I doubt the villagers will fight. If I have to do this alone again, then so be it. It will not be enough to stop me from trying.

My sword trembles in my hand as I slow my pace. I need to conserve my energy, take them out one at a time. The last thing I need is to be cornered. My breastplate ripples against my movements, a strange sensation after so long trapped within it. I hope it will still be enough to protect me.

The first creature that I stumble across has already made it within the walls of the town. It stands tall, digging one of its razor sharp pincers into the roof of a house as though trying to tear it off. I raise my sword and run in to stop it. There could be children under that roof. They must be terrified out of their wits. I grit my teeth and swing my sword, slicing right into the leg of the creature.

Relief floods through me as the creature's limb detaches, sending the monstrous beast toppling onto its back. Killing Laurel worked. Or perhaps it is the magic laced in the sword that killed it. I do not know which and I do not care. I have no time to worry about it, so I leap onto the creature's upturned belly and plunge my sword into it. When the creature stops thrashing, I keep going, making my way to the border.

The creature climbing the wall looms tall over me as I reach it. I gasp as it launches itself at me, rolling sideways to avoid being crushed by it. The creature's crash landing at least offers me a moment to gather my wits, giving me the chance to run in and end its life.

I whip my head around to see where trouble might appear from next. I catch sight of a civilian hiding behind his curtains, watching me fight. I cannot even be angry at his cowardice. I am full of fear too. But I allow it to fuel me as I run to the kingdom's gate to see what waits beyond.

It is like going back in time. I watch as the creatures arrive in force, appearing over the hills for what feels like miles around. My heart squeezes when I realize they have likely come from their massacre at Deepmoat. Laurel's work has destroyed an entire kingdom.

But it won't destroy this one.

I am not just fighting to save my kingdom anymore. As I run into the fray and slash down each monster, I hold on to hope. Hope that after this is over, there might be something waiting for me. That maybe it is not too late for me. That maybe I am worthy of happiness, of love, of a new start. I cry out as my sword swishes and slices, a deadly dance through the fields where my mother and father fell. But this time, there are no bodies lying dormant beneath my feet. I may be alone in this fight once again, but no one dies today. Not without taking me down first.

My shoulders ache with the effort of the fight as the battle continues. Four, five, six of the creatures fall, but they are coming faster than I can cope with. Many surpass me entirely, heading to the wall to destroy the town. I know I need to fall back, but the moment I do, more will come. I am panting for breath, taking each monster as it comes, but it is becoming clear to me that I need to do something more to stop the horde. Sweat is dripping from my forehead. Exhaustion is hitting me hard. I suppose three years of no sleep and no food are catching up to me. My humanity is everything I desired, but now, it limits me.

And as tiredness hits, mistakes are made. A slice from a pincer opens a wound on the back of my sword hand. I lose my grip on my sword and it clatters to the ground. I am quick to pick it back up, but as the wound on my hand tugs itself open like a budding flower, it becomes more painful to grip my sword. I grit my teeth and carry on. *It is only pain. The pain cannot kill you,* I tell myself. But even as I am trying to regain my stance in the battle, a creature tramples right over me, one of its feet crushing my chest and forcing me to the ground. My eyes widen and I gasp for air, wondering if this is it. Its body blocks my entire vision, an obsidian cloud above my head. Will it end like this?

Not if I can help it.

The creature moves on, the weight of it leaving my chest. I stand again, winded, but miraculously alive. My breastplate is dented, but my spirit is not. I have something to fight for now.

I come back with feverish desperation, making reckless moves that start to pay off. I run directly beneath one creature, no longer afraid as I end it. I move backward as it falls down, avoiding its crushing weight, and begin a new strategy. I work my way back toward the city walls, taking anything down that comes in my way. It will not work forever. If I do not figure out how to stop them quicker, the town will be overwhelmed and so will I. But as long as I still have life left inside me, I will keep them at bay.

At the gate, I make my final stand. Gripping my sword, my hands coated in the black blood of the monsters, I watch them come for me. An endless sea of black spiders, all of them ready to kill me. My lungs shudder as I try to find air. I hold my sword tighter and say a prayer to the goddess. *Selene, save me. Or at least make my passing swift.* I swallow back my fear and watch death come at me face on. They are meters away. I take a deep breath.

And then I hear the voice of an angel.

"Stay away from her!"

I look to my left and see her riding in on a white horse, her eyes alight with gold. Fiora's forehead is creased with fury, and I watch her raise her hands to unleash it all upon the monsters. My heart lifts in my chest. I have been offered a second chance. Selene heard my cry.

And Fiora has returned to me.

I do not know how she made it here, or how she has come to my rescue, but I decide not to question a miracle. I have a new found courage, a new found strength. My sword feels weightless as I begin to fight once more. The creatures crash into battle with undeniable strength, strength that I cannot compete with.

But Fiora can. I see her fire unleashed, raining down upon them before they can get too close. My sword feels feeble in comparison, but it does the job. I leap back into the fray, making myself of use. Fire swallows up all of the air on the battlefield, making it hard to breathe, but my heart is on fire too. It keeps me moving. Now, I push back into the field, edging the wall of enemies further away from Thornwood. It is slow progress, but with Fiora riding through, taking down whole ranks of the arachnid army, I watch the battle turn in our favor.

I hear the howl of a wolf and turn, my heart seizing in my chest. I see Bolt running toward me, Sigrid perched upon her back. Sigrid salutes me, her lute in her other hand. Bolt stops only to allow her to get off her back and then she runs to me, her white fur whipping in the wind. Tears burn my eyes. I thought I might never see her again.

I fall to my knees and allow her to jump into my arms. I forget the war raging behind me. My heart is bursting with love, love that was forced beneath the surface for far too long. Bolt licks my face and I know she is glad to see me. When I pull away, she lets out a staccato bark before running into the battle. I gather myself as I hear the music of Sigrid's lute begin to play, my sword back in my hand. But even as I stand, I see that the force of Fiora's arrival is incomparable. Our foes fall all around us, burning hot under her raging fire.

I slash and stab my way toward her. After all we have been through, I cannot leave her alone in the battle, even if she does not need me. My strength is nothing compared to her's, but I will protect her with my life if I must.

My wounds are plenty now and I am clinging on to my last remnants of strength, but even as I fall apart, so do the enemy. They still come at us, hard and fast, but now, there is hope. With Fiora, with Bolt, with Sigrid, we are more evenly matched.

The battle becomes a blur. My sword slashes until my shoulder feels that it might come out of its socket. I feel the sting of a thousand cuts, stray pincers clawing at me and leaving their mark, but I barely notice. I have too much hope inside me to give in to a few scratches. My sword leads the way even as my body begins to falter. This can be over soon. This can be it forever.

I just have to push.

And then, all at once, it feels as though there are only a few left. Weariness tugs at me, trying to make me fall down, but I resist as hard as I can. Only a little longer, and I can rest. I can tell Fiora how glad I am to see her. I can…

Fiora's fire comes to a sudden stop. I turn to see what the problem is. Her skin is covered in a sheen of sweat, her eyelids drooping. I can see the exhaustion on her face, the twinkle in her eyes burned out. My mouth falls open as I watch her body turn limp and she falls from her horse.

I run before she can hit the ground, half catching her as I fall to my knees, her body light as a feather in my arms. Her eyelids are flickering. She is very much alive, but exhaustion has taken her. She breathes raspily and panic takes hold in my chest. We need her. The battle is not yet won.

I turn and see four more creatures coming for us. Sigrid, still perched upon on the wall, is too far away for her music to sway them. Bolt is some way away, taking down the dregs that remain. It falls to me to take these on. I turn back to Fiora, pressing a kiss to her forehead desperately.

"Don't fade away, my fallen star," I whisper. I lay her gently on the ground and turn to the creatures, my sword drawn one final time. If they want her, they will have to get through me first. I would rather die than see her hurt.

My body feels heavy, but I steel myself and rush into the fight once again. I dodge a pincer and dive beneath the creature that attacked me, but instead of going for the kill, I come out the other side. The four of them clump together, so desperate to swipe at me that their bodies clash with one another. It gives me a chance to cripple two of them, my sword swinging in a wide arc that takes out three limbs in one go. A I feel a sharp pain in my arm as something attacks me in the chaos, but I grit my teeth and whip around to assess the situation.

As two of them fall, one seems to have the sense to scurry away, making for Fiora. Before it can get far, I launch myself up onto its leg and clamber up its body to make a killing blow between the eyes. The creature topples sideways and I allow myself to fall with it, hitting the ground and rolling away with a clank of armor.

Pain shoots through my wounded arm, but I push through it. I move as quickly as I can, returning to put the two crippled monsters out of their misery.

And with that, only one remains.

The final one is moving for Fiora's still body. I will not reach it in time to stop its deadly pincers, unless I stand in its way. Tears sting my eyes. I have nothing left to give, but my life. If that is the price to keep Fiora safe, then consider it paid.

I stagger forward, my sword shaking in my left hand. I can barely hold it. But I have to try. I run as hard as I can and swing my sword, attempting to hit the creature's leg. It hits the target, but not hard enough. It flinches away from my sword, preparing its pincer. I am too slow to move, too weary to stop what I know is coming.

I cry out as the pincer impales my side.

Chapter Fifteen

I fall to the ground, holding my breath as though to prolong the moment before the pain sets in. But when it does, it is agony. The pincer punctured right through my armor, leaving me with a hole in my side. Now, my breaths come too fast, my eyes widening.

I know there is no coming back from this.

My vision blurs and my head hits the ground as I lose the war to stay upright. I want to call out to Fiora, to Bolt, but the pain is so severe that I cannot even scream. All I can do is try to focus on breathing, on staying alive just a little longer.

I hear a screech from the creature nearby. No doubt someone has finished what I started. Tears of relief escape from my eyes. If the creature is dead then Fiora should survive. That is all that matters.

An anguished howl from nearby lets me know that Bolt has found me. Her fur brushes my face as she collapses beside me, whimpering. I lean my face into her. The pain eases a little with her beside me.

"It will be okay, Bolt. The world does not end with me," I whisper. There are worse places to die than beside my truest friend. I cannot move to stroke her, to let her know that I am not yet gone. I let my tears fall silently, each breath I take becoming more of a struggle.

"Alana!"

Her voice brings life back to me for a moment. I felt I was about to slip away. I feel something pulling at me and my head rests upon something new. When I open my eyes, Fiora looks down at me, tears escaping her beautiful eyes.

"Alana, do not slip away. I am not done with you yet," she chokes, her chest shuddering as she sobs. I look up at her, dazed as my life seems to slip through my fingers. The world has slowed now, and the pain has numbed. There is peace in knowing she is okay. That my death will mean something.

"It is alright…"

"No. It will never be alright again," she whispers. "But I told you. I am not done with you."

"Just grant me one last thing," I murmur, my eyes closing. "Kiss me. I want your lips to be the last thing I know. Please, Fiora. It is my only wish."

Her hands are trembling as she cups my face. I manage to open my eyes one final time. I watch her lean in, her lips ready to greet my own.

I kiss her with everything I have left, and I know that if I could survive this moment, I would never be the same. I have been touched by gold now and it fills me with the feeling of a thousand sparkling stars. But she is the only star that matters to me. Her kiss tastes how I imagine magic should - sweet as honey, sharp as a lightning bolt, hot as the summer sun. It is everything I ever wanted it to be. And even as my eyes flutter closed, even as my life leaves me, I know I have experienced true perfection with my dying breath.

And then I let go.

I expect to wake up in the arms of the goddess. I expect to be guided into her heavenly lands to live in fields of green, in a place with no pain, no heartache, no anger left in my heart.

I wake in my old bedroom.

As my eyes flutter open, I stare up at the ceiling, feeling as though I cannot move yet. I wonder what is wrong with me. Am I in a coma? Is this all just some dream I am locked in, some place between death and living?

But slowly, sensation returns to me. I can feel a dull ache where I was stabbed in my side and in my right arm. I can feel warm sunlight coming in through the window. There is a twist of hunger in my stomach and my tongue is dry. These are things I have not felt in so long that I almost forgot their sensations.

I am alive.

I do not understand how this is possible. Slowly, I manage to sit up. I am no longer wearing my heavy armor, changed instead into a cotton nightdress. I can feel the bindings of a bandage around my stomach, but I am not in as much pain as I should be. I blink several times to adjust to the light and find that Bolt is sleeping close to me, her snout resting on her paws and her ears sagging. I want to reach out and stroke her fur, but I fear I will disturb her.

And then I spot that we are not alone.

On the floor at the foot of my bed, Fiora sleeps, her head resting on the mattress. My heart floods with warmth. I cannot believe she is here, that she stayed beside me this whole time. I thought I would never see her again.

And then I remember our kiss. How it felt like the end of everything. But now, I wonder if it was only the beginning. If this is real, if I have survived my darkest day…then maybe I can begin again.

"Fiora?"

Her eyes flutter open slowly, like she is unsure why she is being coaxed from her dreams. She wipes sleep from her eyes, turning her head slowly to look at me. Then realization sets in. Her mouth forms a smile. The twinkle returns to her eyes.

"Oh my goodness...Alana..."

She almost trips in her haste to get to her feet and then her arms are around me, holding me delicately until I pull her harder against me, ignoring the pain in my side. It is worth it. All this time, there has been a barrier between us, my armor keeping her from ever getting close. Now, I crush her to my chest, my emotions raw and wild. This is what I have been missing for so long. This is what I have craved. I lost so much to make it to this moment, but I would do it all again, just to get me here.

Fiora pulls away and cups my face, her eyes softening. "I was so worried about you."

"How is this real? How am I here?" I blink several times. "Did your kiss save me?"

Fiora grins. "I cannot claim to have that power within me. Love cannot fix all. No, I healed you with a strong potion."

"But your brews are horrendous..."

"I do not appreciate your jibe. But I did not

make it. Petra gifted it to me. She said I would need it. That your stubbornness would get you killed. It takes years to brew a potion so strong…but fortunately, Petra has been busy over the years."

"Dark magic," I murmur. "Petra said that there is no way to save someone from death without it."

"Yes, that is true," Fiora says, stroking my cheek. "But in this case…we both agreed it was worth it."

I let that sink in. Petra's reluctance to turn back to dark magic makes guilt stab at my sides. If she offered up this potion, then she must have been truly certain that she did not want me to die.

"She really gave that to you? To save me?"

Fiora's eyes soften. "All this time, you have been running around saving everyone else. Petra knew you deserved to be saved this time around."

The notion makes me feel so tired. I am not sure what I deserve. So many years of my life were lost to helping those who did not deserve it, and it twisted me up inside. That does not make me feel deserving of mercy.

But Fiora's touch makes the thought drift away like a fading bad dream. She is here now. That is worth every minute I spent alone, wishing for someone like her to come to my side. I take her hand in mine, brushing the pad of my thumb over her skin.

"How did you make it to us in time? To save us, to join the battle?"

"I stole a horse," she admits with a sheepish grin. "And I rode as hard as I could. When I got close to the borders, I had to fight my way in through the back to get to you. Did you truly believe that I left with the intention of not returning? I had no plans to allow you to have your way back in Shadowwater. But I left because I knew that was what you needed of me. And I knew by the time I returned, you would have had enough time to see where you went wrong." She pauses, her gaze falling to her lap. "I knew there were some things you needed to do. Things that did not involve me."

"I am so sorry I sent you away," I whisper. "I thought…I never expected that I would make it out alive. I just wanted you to be safe. I wanted-"

She cuts me off with a kiss that takes my breath away. Our first kiss was desperate, a final grasp at the life I always wanted. This one feels like raw passion. Fiora's breath is hot on mine, her delicate hand gripping my hair. For the first time, my hands go to touch her with no tentativeness, tugging her waist to pull her onto my lap. My hands find her beautiful face, thumbs stroking her cheeks as I cherish my first true kiss with her. She breaks away from the kiss and nuzzles into my neck, gently kissing the skin just below my ear. My skin tingles, still getting used to sensation at all, let alone something so intense. I breathe into Fiora's shoulder, her golden tattoos glowing on the exposed skin of her collarbone, her neck, her chest. She is so radiant that I can barely believe she would want to touch a monster like -

I pull away from her. Fiora's brow creases.

"Is everything alright? Did I hurt you? I am so sorry, I only wanted to show you that you have nothing to be sorry for…"

"It is not that," I murmur. She shifts off my lap and I stand shakily, limping my way over to the dusty mirror on the opposite side of the room.

For the first time in three years, I see my body unobstructed, with only a thin nightgown to cover me. Shakily, my hands run over the shape of me. I feel the softness of my belly for the first time since my breastplate was removed. I run my hands over my burly arms that I have told myself are far too big, unbecoming for a woman. I pinch at the folds of skin between my arms and my chest and wish them away as I have so many times before.

And then there is my face. The deep scars that run over it now, some new, some old. I tell myself that it has marred any beauty I could possess if I tried a little harder to present like other women.

I never felt like I quite made sense to everyone around me. Though I craved the idea of pretty dresses and flowers in my hair, I never imagined I was built to enjoy them like the other girls. I was often told I was too loud, too boisterous, too much. So I took those words to heart and became what they said I was. And the day I was cursed, it only solidified me as the beast they wanted me to be. To help them process me for what I was, to fit into their idea of who they believed me to be.

It occurs to me now that the hate I have for myself runs deep. I look at my reflection and I push myself to go beyond the things I pick up on first. I tell myself that my teeth are too crooked. That the hair on and beneath my arms is unsightly. That my skin could be smoother, that my feet should be more dainty, that my thick eyebrows turn heads for all the wrong reasons. I tell myself that I am a joke that the rest of the world is laughing at except for me.

Once, a long time ago, I looked at this body and felt nothing close to hate. I did not love myself the way that I should, but I did not flinch at my reflection.

But in the last three years, it has been impossible to ignore the voices. The crowds of people in my kingdom hurling hate my way. The voices inside my head winning out in a battle of self-loathing. I took the words of those who hated me most and pinned them to my skin until I saw only how they described me. *Monster. Beast. Abomination.* Those words belonged to them first. But then I made them my own until I saw little of the woman I once was, the woman I could have been, the woman I wished I was.

I know that their hatred went beyond what they saw on the outside, that it was rooted in something deeper, but Fiora was right. Out of all those voices shouting at me, my own was the loudest and most hateful.

"Alana?"

Tears prick my eyes. Fiora tentatively approaches me and stands behind me in the mirror, her tall frame level with mine. Her hands find my arms and begin to rub them until I let go of some of the tension I am holding in my body.

"I understand what you may be thinking about," she murmurs. "You have treated yourself with such unkindness for so long that you are wary of my affections. Is that true?"

I swallow back tears and nod. She sees right through me. Her hands grip me tight, a gentle reminder that she is here with me.

"I wish that you could see yourself as I do. The way I have since we met. I know you had no intentions of letting me get close, but I saw through the cracks in your facade. And I fell in love with you. Not just for what I see inside you, but what is on the outside. You are so beautiful, Alana. Hair the color of wine…eyes so blue that I think of the ocean each time I see you. A body both strong and soft. A body I want to love and to cherish. And your face…those scars may have changed you, but never for the worse. They are not the imperfections you believe them to be. Do not listen to how the world screams at you and makes you feel unloved. Listen to me. Listen to what your heart tells you, deep down. I want you to feel loved, because you are. And someday…I want you to love yourself."

I close my eyes for a minute, gathering courage within myself, and then look in the mirror again. My breath hitches as I see myself in a new light. And of course, Fiora is right. All these things I have damned myself for over the years are strengths, not weaknesses. I am nothing like the person I see myself as. I am brave. I am fierce. I am different, but I am not ugly, beastly, monstrous. I can still be the woman I wanted to be when I was trapped inside a cage of thorns. I can still move on and be happy.

And yes, I am imperfect. I have a lot of rage inside me that I want to quell. I have done things that make me scared of what I might become. If I could turn back time, there are things I would do differently.

And yet, had things been different, I may not be standing here now. The past is in the past. Now, I have a chance to write the tale of my future. I turn and find Fiora's hands, squeezing them gently.

"I need some time. To understand myself, to learn the path I want to walk. But I love you. And whichever path I choose, I want to take it with you."

Fiora's eyes fill with tears, but she smiles at me. "And I will follow wherever you want to go."

Our lips meet again. Gently, this time. I close my eyes and savor the moment. Love is all I ever wanted, all I ever needed to navigate my way through life. And now that it has found me, I know that everything will be okay. There will be tougher days. Healing will not be easy.

But for the first time, I will not have to do this all alone.

Chapter Sixteen

Fiora insists that I stay in bed for a few days to ensure I am fully healed and to allow the potion to do its work. I spend my time with her and Bolt, learning how to sleep and eat again. Once I get a taste for food, Neville starts bringing me all sorts of delicacies - flaky pork pies, cuts of honeyed bacon, spiced sausages, plates of boiled potatoes in butter, vegetable stew with hunks of bread, legs of chicken. It turns out he really is quite the cook, or perhaps it is just the reawakening of my tastebuds. I had forgotten how good it feels to not just eat, but savor food. And for once, I do not worry that it is unladylike to eat so much, or that it will gain me weight. I enjoy every mouthful, considering it a part of my rebirth. From now on, I am practicing being kinder to myself and to my body. It is easier said than done, but I will succeed.

Sleep comes easily now as well. I slip into it

and dream of all the good that I have in my life. I imagined I would be haunted by everything I have been through, but it all feels like a distant memory now, even though I am only just leaving it behind. I prefer it this way. I do not have to worry any longer.

But as my strength returns, I begin to question how I will move forward in this life. On the first day that I am allowed out of bed, I leave my friends behind to walk in my rose garden. The weather has cleared, sunshine peeking through clouds of gray as I walk by the rose bushes. I stop to pluck a rose and catch my finger on a thorn, wincing. But even as blood appears on my finger, I smile. I am lucky to be free of my curse, to feel everything in full once again. I am lucky for a lot of things.

But there is the matter of my future. I still rule a kingdom of people who hate me. And yes, Fiora is here with me now, but I know she will not want to stay here. She is a free spirit, destined to keep exploring the world, seeing everything she can with her friends. We have not spoken about it, but I sense how much she itches to keep moving. She has been in one place for far too long.

I do not want to lose her. After so long on my own, my only true desire is to be with the woman I love. But I know that to do that, I have to leave this place.

I search the sky for answers. I know above us all, the goddess Selene watches over us. I never ask her for much. Even in my years of misery alone, I never asked anything of her. But this is my true time of need. I need to know what I can do.

"I cannot be happy here," I whisper. "Thornwood has brought me nothing, but pain. I know that my duty should be enough to keep me here…my people need a queen. But…but does it have to be me? I never wanted this. My people would not miss me. My parents would hate to see me leave…but they are gone. They will never return. So…would it be so wrong to go? To seek something more?"

I wait for answers, my eyes raised to the clouds. Slowly, I watch as they part, the sun beaming stronger than ever before. When I turn, I see that the light has illuminated the land beyond the vine walls. I look beyond and know that my future lies out there. Until a few weeks ago, I had never even seen the ocean. What other wonders have I missed, confined within this place? My chest fills with hope. I smile up at the sky.

"Thank you, goddess," I whisper. I will not let her down. I will live this life as she intended us to - enjoying the beauty of the world she had a hand in creating. Basking in the sun, living off the fruits of the land, feeling the breeze in my hair. Eagerly, I begin to pluck more roses from the bush, gathering them together in a bouquet. It is time that I spoke to Fiora.

It takes me some time to find her, but I have an idea of where she might have gone. She has been spending a lot of time in the raven tower, looking longingly out at the lands beyond Thornwood. I cannot blame her. I know she is staying here for me and me only. I have held her back long enough. The others, too. But it does not have to be that way any longer.

She turns to see me and smiles. I hold the roses behind me, smiling back.

"Did you enjoy your walk?" she asks me.

"I did. In fact, I found it very useful. I consulted with my goddess about something important."

"You did? What might that be?"

"About whether to bring my lady flowers," I tease, showing her the bouquet. She gasps in delight, taking the roses from me and sniffing them.

"They are beautiful, Alana. Thank you. What a wonderful gift."

I pause, feeling a little nervous. "There…there is more."

She raises her eyebrow in surprise. "Oh?"

I step forward and cup her face in my hands. "I have been thinking about my place in the world. I think I have known for a long time that it is not here. I…I intend to leave here. With you."

Fiora's lips part in shock. "Alana…I cannot ask that of you…"

"You do not need to. I want to. And I know that you will never be happy here. You want to see what the world has to offer…and so do I."

"What of your people? Your duty?"

"You said it yourself…these people have no need of me. They only ever called upon me when trouble darkened their doorstep. And now, that part of their life is over. The kingdom is safe once again. If I leave here, they may elect their own queen…someone who shares their values, perhaps. And we can go somewhere that their values do not matter. Maybe someday we can settle someplace where magic is not hated. I do not care where we go…I only want to be at your side."

Fiora slowly smiles, the gold flecks in her eyes shimmering. "Then it is settled. I will take you with me. When shall we go?"

I smile. "As soon as we can. I do not want to waste another minute of this life."

I lean in to kiss Fiora. I shall never get used to the softness of her lips, to the magic that buzzes between us as we share these moments. When we part once again, Fiora is glowing like never before.

"I could not be happier," she whispers. I chuckle.

"Do not say that. There is so much happiness yet to come."

Two days pass before we are all ready to leave. It takes that long for us to pack up the things we want to take with us and for me to say goodbye to Thornwood. I may be keen to leave here, but there are some things that are hard to say goodbye to. This is where my mother and father laid to rest, where I grew up playing in the grounds, where I met Fiora. It is where my library is, the one place that felt like home to me. It is where the presence of Selene is at its strongest, and it feels painful to think of leaving my goddess behind. There is happiness among the pain here, and it is hard to let go of that. I know that once I leave this place, I will never return.

But by the time I close the doors to the castle for the final time, I feel ready. Sigrid and Calla are loading up their horse with supplies, and Neville is packing the food for the first leg of our journey. I do not know where we are headed - I asked for it to be a surprise. But I hear we have a long journey ahead of us.

Bolt is keen to leave, chasing her tail to do something with her energy. Her saddle is ready to go, ready for Fiora and I to ride once again. It is funny how much has changed since our last journey. Now, we are finally together. We are finally happy.

"Alright, we are set!" Neville declares with a wide smile. "Shall we hit the road?"

"Goddess, yes," Sigrid says. "I have never been more ready to move on."

"Me neither," I say. I clamber upon Bolt's back and Fiora slides onto the saddle behind me, wrapping her arms around my waist. I sigh in bliss. There is nothing keeping us apart any longer. No thorned armor to separate us. No curses or wars or dark magic to stand in our way.

"Ready?" I murmur to Fiora. She grips me harder.

"Absolutely," she says. I ruffle Bolt's fur.

"Let's go, Bolt!"

She lets out a wild howl and then begins to run. Fiora laughs as Bolt picks up speed, leaving the others in our dust. I barely bother to look at the townsfolk as we ride past them. They have no power over me any longer. It is time to leave the past behind and focus on my future - my life with Fiora.

We ride into the unknown.

About the Author

HAYLEY ANDERTON is a full time ghostwriter and the author of the YA LGBT romance novel, Double Bluff. She is also the co-author of the Kindle Unlimited series, Apocalypse. When she's not writing she loves to bake and hang out with fluffy friends. For editing services and business enquiries, she can be contacted at hayleyandertonbusiness@gmail.com.

Instagram: @hayley_a_writes
Twitter: @handerton96
Wattpad: @hazzer123

If you enjoyed this novel, please consider reviewing it on Amazon and Goodreads!

More books by the author

All books are available to purchase as paperbacks or ebooks. All books are also enrolled in Kindle Unlimited.

The Last Girls on Earth

Book 1: Sloth
Book 2: Gluttony
Book 3: Greed

Apocalypse Series

Book 1: Apocalypse
Book 2: Fallout
Book 3: Chaos
Book 4: Sacrifice
Book 5: Outlast
Book 6: Alliance

Coming Soon…

The Risen Series

Book 1: The Risen
Book 2: The Lost
Book 3: The Remains

Other Books:

Double Bluff
Homebound

Printed in Great Britain
by Amazon